THE DUTCH BLUE ERROR

William G. Tapply

The Dutch Blue Error is a rare stamp, worth a million dollars because it is supposed to be unique. Then a mysterious caller tells the owner there is a duplicate ... and he must buy it to preserve the value of his own stamp. Lawyer Brady Coyne is called in as go-between. But the simple transaction turns into murder and Brady finds himself not only tracking the killer but protecting a beautiful girl and defending the prime suspect ... all over a tiny piece of paper. The case isn't closed until Brady finds the true nature of that stamp.

The Dutch Blue Error

WILLIAM G. TAPPLY

John Curley & Associates, Inc.
South Yarmouth, Ma.

Library of Congress Cataloging in Publication Data

Tapply, William G.
  The Dutch Blue Error.

  1. Large type books.   I. Title.
[PS3570.A568D8   1985]   813'.54   85–10979
  ISBN 0–89340–937–5

Published in Large Print by arrangement with Charles Scribner's Sons in the U.S.A. and Collins: Publishers in the U.K. and Commonwealth.

Distributed in the U.K. and Commonwealth by Magna Print Books.

Printed in Great Britain

For Mum and Dad

AUTHOR'S NOTE

I wish to thank Rick Boyer and Betsy Rapoport again for their critical and spiritual support; my wife, Cindy, for her uncanny editorial eye as well as her tolerance; and my children, Michael, Melissa, and Sarah, for their patience and encouragement.

THE
DUTCH BLUE
ERROR

PROLOGUE: San Juan, 1967

Guillaume Lundi muttered, *"Merde."* An eight and a five. With a sigh, he crooked his forefinger and beckoned to the dealer. A black queen slid across the green felt table.

Lundi leaned back and rolled his shoulders up along the sides of his neck as his cards and the ten-dollar chip were raked away. He was tired. He wanted only to sleep. And if he had to gamble, he would have preferred roulette, where he could play at nearly fifty-fifty odds.

But his instructions had been clear. They had arrived in the envelope with his round-trip ticket from Paris to San Juan. "Take a cab from the airport to the Hotel Europeana. Deposit the item in the hotel safe. Go directly to the casino. Take a seat at the first blackjack table on the left. Play ten-dollar bets. Wait for Grayson."

He hoped Grayson would show up soon so they could make the transaction quickly. His return-flight ticket was open, and he wanted only to get back to Paris and crawl into his big bed beside his big warm wife and sleep away his travels through time zones and time warps and wake up at 6:30 in the morning. He didn't care what day it might be. But he wanted it to be 6:30 in the morning.

The dealer slipped him a nine, then a six. Lundi put his chip on top of his cards. He'd stay with the fifteen. Lousy cards, but the dealer showed a five. He'd have to take a hit.

The young woman in the seat beside him showed a four and a jack. "Hit me," she said tonelessly, as if she knew she'd lose. When she saw the eight she nodded her head vigorously, acknowledging the inevitable. "Shit," she said loudly, as her last chip was raked away.

"Well," she said, addressing the others at the table, "I quit. That's it for me. Back to the beach."

"Tough luck," said Lundi.

"Yeah," she said, "that's it. Bad luck." She slid out of her seat and wandered away.

A big man with black curly hair on his knuckles took her seat. Like Lundi, he began to play ten-dollar chips. Lundi got a blackjack and won double. He split a pair of nines and lost on both. He stayed on a twelve. It was an unreliable hunch. The dealer's six had a four under it.

The man with the hairy fingers touched his arm. "Mind if I bum a cigarette?" His

2

voice seemed to whisper from somewhere deep inside his big chest.

"*Pas de tout,*" said Lundi, pushing his pack of Marlboros toward the man.

"Thanks a lot." The man had pale green eyes and silver-rimmed glasses and powerful shoulders. His head seemed to squat directly atop those shoulders like a bowling ball on a table. His dark hair was flecked with gray.

"You're Lundi." It was a statement.

"Yes. And you're . . .?"

"Grayson."

"Well," sighed the Frenchman. "Mr. Grayson, finally. I'm glad you're here."

Grayson eyed Lundi's short stack of chips and smiled. "I suppose you are. You have the item?"

"Yes. Of course."

"Well, unless you'd like to continue playing, why don't we get it, then, shall we?"

Lundi picked up his chips, stood, then turned and dropped two of them at his place with a nod to the dealer, who nodded solemnly back at him and raked them in.

They went to the desk in the hotel lobby, where Lundi exchanged a slip of paper for a battered briefcase. Then they entered an elevator and rode up through the bowels of the hotel. They emerged into an empty corridor.

Grayson bent to unlock the door to his room, then pushed it open and stood back to let Lundi in. The room seemed surprisingly small for a luxurious hotel – no larger than the Holiday Inn singles Lundi usually took when he was in America.

Grayson pulled the door shut behind himself and went to the wall-sized window. He drew the heavy curtains shut, then moved to a table that held an assortment of bottles and glasses. He splashed some Scotch into a glass.

"You?" he asked Lundi.

"The same. No ice."

Lundi stood awkwardly for a moment, then sat on the bed and leaned forward slightly, his hands clasped between his legs which dangled just above the floor. He wished Grayson had left the curtains open. He found the big sky and empty, dark ocean a soothing antidote to a hectic day.

Grayson handed Lundi his drink, which he accepted with a murmur and sipped thirstily.

Grayson seemed unable to settle. He moved nervously around the room. He had the quick, agile movements of a boxer, Lundi thought. In spite of his bulk, he was graceful and lithe.

"Would you mind opening the curtains?"

4

"Yes," said Grayson. "I mind." Instead, he picked up a wooden chair and brought it to the side of the bed where the Frenchman sat, twirled it around so that the back faced Lundi, and slid onto it. He crossed his arms over the top of the chair, rested his chin on his thick wrists, and fixed Lundi with a grin. "Okay. Let's see it, then."

Lundi opened the old briefcase and handed an envelope to Grayson, who glanced perfunctorily at its contents, then said, "And the papers?"

Lundi handed him the documents. These the big man scrutinized more carefully. Lundi finished his Scotch and watched Grayson without interest. He wanted to lie back on the bed and sleep. The Scotch burned pleasantly in his stomach. He wanted his big warm wife, whom he would hug from behind, her great soft rump against his stomach, his hand buried between her thighs. He yearned to sleep, and later awaken. She would turn to face him. They would make love then, in their comfortable, practiced way.

". . . trace it? Mr. Lundi?"

"I'm sorry. What was it?"

"I said, you're certain no one can trace it?"

"Oh, yes," sighed Lundi. "Absolutely. I am the only one who knows my client's

5

name. I paid with a cashier's check, as instructed. I told no one. Those people, they understand and respect that. It's not uncommon, the desire for an anonymous transaction. And I, I understand discretion. That, I assume, is why I was retained to perform the service. And now, if everything is in order, I would appreciate your paying me so that I can return to the airport. It has been a long day for me. A very long day."

Grayson rose from the chair. "Why don't you pour us another drink," he said, "while I get you your money."

"*Bon.*" Lundi yawned and got slowly to his feet. He placed the palms of his hands on his lower back and rolled his hips, then moved wearily to the low table where the bottles stood. He splashed some Scotch into his glass. Without turning around, he said to Grayson, "Where's your –"

He never finished the sentence. Grayson's left forearm circled his chest from behind, viselike, pinning his arms and whooshing the breath from his lungs. Lundi gasped. He could not inhale, so insistent was Grayson's embrace.

"So sorry, Mr. Lundi," whispered Grayson into his ear. Lundi felt Grayson's free hand cup his chin. The fingers and thumb caressed the jawbone on either side,

6

feeling for the proper grip. Then Lundi felt his chin suddenly squeezed hard in Grayson's hand. A quick, hard jerk sideways and upward, and Lundi heard, rather than felt, the grinding and popping of cervical vertebrae. He felt his body melt away, drained of life, a moment of tingling and then nothing. The last sensation to register in Guillaume Lundi's brain was the fetid odor of human excrement. Then came the final blackness.

That is how I imagine it happened. Of course, I wasn't there.

What happened afterward, and how I learned Guillaume Lundi's story, and all the deaths that followed years later – those things I can tell you with confidence.

Chapter 1

Oliver Hazard Perry Weston dabbed at his thin, gray mustache with a monogrammed Irish linen table napkin.

"That will be all, Edwin." He nodded to the white-shirted man at his elbow.

"Very good, sir." The gaunt butler disappeared like morning fog.

"Come on, Brady," said Weston to me. "There's something I want to show you."

Perry Weston – Ollie's only son and heir – who was seated at his right, moved quickly to take the handles at the back of his father's wheelchair. Weston flapped the back of his hand at his son without turning around.

"Not you."

Perry jerked his hands away from the wheelchair and held them in front of him in a gesture of mock surrender. Then, with a quick, ironic smile at me, he swiveled around and left the room.

"C'mon, Brady," said Ollie. "Give us a shove, will you?"

"Sure," I replied, taking the handles of his

wheelchair. "Kinda rough on him, weren't you?"

"Nope. He's used to it. Anyway, this is business. For my lawyer, not my son." Ollie raised an aristocratic hand and pointed through the archway and beyond the adjacent living room to a wall of bookshelves that surrounded an enormous fieldstone fireplace.

"The books?"

Ollie nodded.

When I had pushed the old man to the bookcase, he reached up, removed a volume entitled *The Road to Serfdom*, which appeared to be well used, and reached his hand into a vacant space. He fiddled for a moment with what I guessed was a combination lock against the back of the bookcase. Then I heard the faint whine of a motor, and slowly the bookcase slid away into the wall, opening into a smaller room. "In," ordered Weston. I pushed him in.

The wall eased shut behind us. I looked around. We were alone in a windowless room perhaps twenty feet square. Bookshelves, lined with rich, old-looking volumes, covered an entire wall. In one corner a portable bar with shelves of bottles and glittering glassware. In another corner was a giant rolltop desk, which I took to be an antique.

9

Across another wall hung a row of mounted heads: an eland, an elk, a tawny cat which I guessed was some kind of panther, a sheep with huge, curled horns, an antelope. Against the same wall stood a glass-fronted gun cabinet, and aligned beneath the glassy-eyed heads were a series of matched prints in silver frames. I leaned closer to study them and saw they weren't prints at all, but original watercolors. Grouse shooting in Scotland, quail rising before a brace of pointing setters, geese setting their wings to join a set of decoys, woodcock fluttering above New England alders.

"They're nice," I said. "Didn't know you were a hunter, Ollie."

"Was," said Ollie, slapping his dead thighs with his right hand. "Damn good one, too."

"I doubt it not," I murmured.

"So, Counselor. Welcome to my vault." Ollie hoisted himself from his wheelchair onto a dark leather sofa. In front of the sofa stood a low coffee table. The sofa faced a blank, wood-paneled wall. "Fix us a brandy, will you? And let's have a cigar."

I obeyed. Ollie Weston was accustomed to being obeyed, and I understood that. It was a small price to pay for the lucrative opportunities O. H. P. Weston made available to his personal attorney. For his many business dealings, Weston employed large and prestigious law firms. For his private affairs, he employed Brady L. Coyne, and if it fell short of my old dream of arguing the great ethical issues of the day before what FDR called – how times change! – the "nine old men" of the Supreme Court, the retainers and fees of a few wealthy clients like Ollie Weston kept me comfortably ensconced in a nice apartment overlooking the Boston Harbor, and allowed me to fish for trout in places like Newfoundland and New Zealand and Argentina just about whenever I chose to take a vacation – not to mention Gloria's alimony payments, the mortgage on our – her – house in Wellesley, and the college fund for Billy and Joey. So I didn't really mind fetching brandy and cigars for Ollie Weston. It was a small price to pay.

I handed Ollie his drink and cigar, retrieving one of each for myself, and joined the older man on the sofa. Weston leaned back, exhaling a long plume of bluish smoke which seemed to disappear into the ceiling. I looked around the room again. I could detect no source of light. There were no lamps, no evidence of translucent panels from behind which bulbs might glow, and yet the room seemed suffused in a light whiter than sunshine and cleaner and purer

11

than normal artificial light. There were no windows. And I sensed air in motion, although the room appeared to be airtight.

I glanced at Ollie, who was watching me with a faint smile curling on his thin, bloodless lips.

"What do you think, Counselor?"

"You called it a vault."

"And so it is. A giant safe. Fireproof, independent energy source, computerized humidity and temperature control, sterilized air. The entire house could be burning to the ground around us right this minute and we'd never know it. Nor should we care. We'd be perfectly safe. It's totally impenetrable."

I nodded. "It figures."

Ollie laughed, the short chuckle from deep in the throat of a man who expects to surprise people. "It does figure, doesn't it? A man must have a place for his treasures, after all. One certainly can't trust the banks."

I smiled at his joke. Ollie Weston was trustee of Boston's oldest and largest banking house.

He waved his hand around the room. "And these are all treasures, Brady. The books. First editions, many of them several hundred years old. Priceless. I carry not a penny of insurance on them. And the guns.

12

They are irreplaceable. And safer here than in Fort Knox."

He picked up a small metal box from the coffee table in front of him and punched a button. Instantly the wood panels of the blank wall facing the sofa slid back to reveal a giant television screen. Ollie tapped the button again, and the screen began to glow. His eyes glittered.

"In the old days I hunted," he said. "I've killed the biggest game on six continents. I shot German bombers out of the sky over Spain in 1936, when I was a lad of twenty. No quarry was too dangerous, too challenging." He lifted his eyebrows. "And now look at me. Reduced to this." He dropped his hands onto his wasted, motionless legs. "Ironic, eh? I've stood up to the charge of a wounded Cape buffalo, held my ground at the fifty-millimeter cannon when the Stukas came strafing – and what gets me? Some goddam virus you need a microscope to see, gnawing away at my spine."

I sipped my brandy and said nothing. After a moment Ollie smiled and said, "So. Let's play."

He again touched the metal box in his hand. Instantly the giant television screen came to life and a beeping *wock-a-wock-a* kind of music filtered through the room. A grid appeared, and I recognized the grinning yellow head of Pac-Man and the multi-colored ghosts flitting around.

"Aw, come on, Ollie," I protested.

"You never play Pac-Man?"

"Why, sure but . . ."

"So let's play," ordered Oliver Hazard Perry Weston.

Ollie Weston played the video game the way he did everything else: with absolute concentration and total dedication to victory. He hunched forward in the sofa, his long fingers moving swiftly, commanding the little yellow apparition on the screen through the mazes, eating dots, chasing and destroying the little ghosts. The numbers mounted, bells rang, the *wock-a wock-a* music became frenetic. Weston's jaws bulged, and his eyes narrowed with effort. From his throat rose grunts of exertion, growls of disgust, sighs of triumph. When he finally sat back, perspiration beaded his forehead. I noticed that his fingers trembled.

"Beat that," he commanded.

With a shrug I took the metal box into my hand. I tried. I was no match for the old man, as I'm sure he expected. "You win," I said, when my Pac-Man was destroyed for the last time.

We both sat back into the leathery folds

of the sofa for a moment, relit the cigars clenched between our teeth. Without sitting up, Ollie said, "I said I had something to show you."

"So you did."

"Third shelf, fourth from the left."

I went to the bookshelf and removed a thin volume bound in soft beige tooled leather that felt like pigskin. There was no writing on the binding or the cover. I brought it back and handed it to Ollie. He opened it onto his lap.

"I give you," he announced as if he were unveiling the Mona Liza, "the Netherlands fifteen-cent 1852 imperforate. Better known as the Dutch Blue Error."

He regarded me expectantly.

The volume he held open contained one page, a transparent plastic sandwich between the sheets of which was a small, unattractive square of paper. I stared at the postage stamp.

It was a dark, dull blue color with a heavy black postmark on the upper right corner. It had squared-off sides, as if its edges had been trimmed carelessly with scissors. The right profile of a bearded man with a high forehead and a sort of page-boy haircut stared off the side of the stamp. The face was framed by a scrolled oval. In the upper left

15

corner appeared the word *post* and in the upper right *zegel*. In the lower left was a digit *15*, and the lower right held the letter *C*.

It was clearly very old, and otherwise it was totally undistinguished. I glanced at Ollie. He was staring intently at me. A grin played at the corners of his mouth.

I shrugged, smiled, looked back at the stamp, and said, "Yeah?"

"You're not impressed."

"It's very nice. A real nice one, Ollie."

Weston's eyes shifted. They no longer smiled. "Don't patronize me, Brady Coyne. If you don't know philately, that's okay. But don't humor me."

"Sorry. I guess I don't know philately."

"I paid two hundred and twenty-nine thousand dollars for this portrait of King William III. It's the only one of its kind in the world. It could bring a million dollars on the market today."

"It *is* a nice one," I said. I smiled at him so that he could see I was contrite.

He rubbed his thumb across the plastic sheet protecting his prize. He seemed to caress the stamp.

"The Blue Error," he said, as if addressing the stamp. "Discovered in 1885 by a Dutch lad by the name of Hans Wilhelm Van Gluckmann among the papers of his

16

grandfather. Young Hans knew something of stamps – an instance of a little knowledge not being enough, in his case, because he sold it to a dealer who had advertised for the fifteen-cent 1852 issue. The dealer was suspicious, of course, since he knew that the stamps he wanted to purchase were supposed to be orange. But he dipped the blue stamp in water, and when the ink didn't run, he reluctantly upheld his part of the bargain, and young Hans returned home happily with his ten guldens. Typical story. The stamp has changed hands several times. Its full value has never really been realized." Ollie turned his head to look hard at me. "The next time it is sold, it will bring full value. It is a genuine rarity. A priceless treasure. And," he added, touching my knee, "it's mine."

"I used to collect stamps," I said. "When I was a kid. I had several thousand from all over the world. Fascinating hobby. From places like French Equatorial Africa and the Gold Coast and Ceylon, countries that don't even exist any more. Beautiful things. Colorful birds, maps, kings, athletes. I sold my collection so I could buy a motor scooter when I was fifteen. Got sixty-five bucks for it."

Ollie chuckled. "The man who bought it was probably doing you a favor. Listen. I still collect stamps. It's more than a hobby. It's a passion and an investment. Most of my stamps are drab. They're all very old. My total collection numbers forty-seven. Forty-seven stamps. Total." He pushed his face at me. "My stamp collection is worth, conservatively, five point six million dollars."

I shook my head and whistled softly.

"And the Dutch Blue Error," he continued, "is my prize. It has become the mystery stamp of the philatelic world. I have not exhibited it or loaned it to museums or permitted it to be photographed. I have not acknowledged that I own it. I have encouraged romantic legends about my stamp to circulate. That it was seized and held ransom by Irish terrorists and then burned when their hideout was stormed. That the Central Committee of the Soviet Union has it in a vault in the Kremlin. That a crackpot millionaire buried it in his backyard before he died, leaving a treasure map as yet undiscovered. That a beautiful lady ate it when she discovered its owner, her husband, in bed with her sister. Every serious philatelist in the world would kill to own the Dutch Blue Error."

I looked at Ollie sharply. He held up his hand and laughed. "Not literally, of course. My point is this. There are several unique

18

stamps. One-of-a-kind. All, obviously, equally rare, in equally scarce supply. And yet their value ranges from a bit over a hundred thousand to, as I estimate in the case of my little jewel, something over one million dollars."

"I don't get it," I said. "Why...?"

"Why are some worth so much more than others?" Ollie leaned forward, his hands gripping his lifeless knees. "Demand," he whispered. "Demand, Brady. The other half of the economic equation. Listen. The British Guyana one-cent black and magenta – everybody's heard of the black and magenta – it brought a cool eight hundred and fifty thousand back in 1980. Now, that's a unique stamp. Worth an easy million today. But there are other unique stamps, as I told you. The Gold Coast provisional of 1883, for example, or the four-penny Cape of Good Hope Woodblock *tête-bêche*. Or any of the several American Postmaster provisionals – the Alexandria Blue Boy, or the Boscowan, or the Lockport. All of them are just as rare as the black and magenta. What do you suppose those stamps are worth?"

"Jeez, I don't know, Ollie. I guess..."

"I'll tell you." He held up his hand imperiously. "The Lockport Postmaster's Provisional earned its owner a neat twenty-

19

three grand back in 1964. Today? Maybe five times that amount. A bit short of a million, what? The Blue Boy – this is a famous stamp, mind you – the Blue Boy was purchased for eighteen-five in 1967. Now do you see?"

I looked at him. "No. Not really."

"Jesus, Brady. Listen to me. Demand, see? Supply makes value possible. But it's demand that determines it. And demand is something that can be controlled, nurtured. In the world of rare stamps, that is done by myth and legend. Some stamps simply acquire an aura, a mystique. Some never do. Demand is what makes the black and magenta so much more valuable than the others. And the mystique creates that demand. It's what's made my own Dutch Blue Error the equal of the black and magenta."

"What's the mystique, as you call it, of this black and magenta, then?"

"Oh, nothing dramatic. Just that it's universally known as the world's rarest stamp. A misnomer, as I've explained. All unique stamps are obviously equally rare. But the black and magenta was the first truly valuable stamp – the first to bring a big price. It's probably the only stamp that the lay public might recognize. It's ugly as sin. Terrible condition. Its corners have been cut off, and its surface has been rubbed. Somehow that seems to have contributed to its mystique." He shrugged. "You can't always explain mystique. It's like charisma in politicians. Some just seem to have it naturally. Some are able to have it created for them. And some never have a chance for it."

I nodded uncertainly. "And you're creating it for the Dutch Blue Error."

"Yes," he said. He reached over and tapped my leg. "Only four people in this entire world know that I own the Dutch Blue Error. Therein lies its mystery. If the world knew, the myth would be shattered. So would the value of my stamp."

He pointed at the big rolltop desk. "Top left-hand drawer."

I rose and went to the desk, slid open the drawer, and removed an envelope from the top of a stack of papers.

"This?"

Ollie nodded.

"Open it," he said.

I found a single typewritten sheet of paper. I glanced at the bottom and saw no signature, no name. I read it.

"My dear Mr. Weston," it began.

I have in my possession a small blue square of paper 130 years old that I believe will be of interest to you. I assure you it is authentic. This is no hoax. I have chosen to withhold knowledge of my find from the public for the moment on the assumption that it will be to our mutual benefit.

If you do not reply in the precise manner I shall indicate within fourteen days of the postmark on this envelope, I shall be forced to make public my possession of this scrap of paper. Please, therefore, place in the Boston *Globe* automobile classified advertising section the following notice: WANTED: blue '52 Mercedes for collection. Call 922-5518.

Renew the advertisement each day until you hear from me.

My price is £250,000. That is firm. I know you will agree that it is reasonable. Unless you are prepared to pay, do not bother to reply.

"He's got a duplicate of your stamp?" I said.
 "So it would appear."
 "But how? I thought you said..."
 "That mine was one-of-a-kind. Yes. So I thought. For over a hundred years it was

the only one extant. And now?" Ollie shrugged.

"Is it a fake?"

He ran his fingers through his hair and shook his head. "Could be. I tend to doubt it. It's practically impossible to fake something like this. In the first place, he's got nothing to copy it from. And anyway, the state of the art is damn sophisticated nowadays. They can test stamps for age, match the grain of the paper, watermarks, cancellations, the ink, all of it. I can believe he's got the stamp, and that it's real."

"But how? Where did it come from?"

"Your guess is as good as mine, my friend," sighed the old man. "Somebody's attic, probably, or a trunk in a barn. Somebody's grandmother's old love letters. A rusty old strongbox full of old bills and receipts. Who knows? The point is, he's got it."

"Okay. But why all this subterfuge?"

"You haven't been listening to me. Let me try it again. Okay? First, what determines the value of the stamp?"

"It's rarity. Aha, and the mystery. No one knows you own it."

"Good. Now, by induction, my boy, what happens to the value of my unique stamp if another suddenly appears?"

"Obviously it's reduced."

"Reduced! Ha! It's destroyed Annihilated, Brady. So therefore, by the same logic, what is the value of the duplicate of my stamp on the open market?"

"Not much, I guess."

"Good. Right. But for whom *does* it have value?"

"You?"

"Me. Right. Of course. This fellow knows that. He knows that I will pay what the open market will not pay, because the stamp is worth infinitely more to me than to anyone else. I want that stamp, Brady. I will pay the man his price."

"A quarter of a million dollars? Jesus, Ollie."

"That is what the man says here. For two hundred and fifty thousand I will own the stamp, protect my investment, and purchase this man's sworn secrecy. I know he understands all of that."

I thought about it for a moment. "Why doesn't this guy sell his stamp as if it were the one you own? You know, as if *it* were the unique Dutch Blue Error?"

"Only a fair question, my friend. Not a good one. First, I doubt he has papers of authentication – that trace the various sales and so forth of the stamp, along with the

24

appraisal of a recognized authority that the stamp isn't a fake, that it is what it purports to be. Without those papers, his stamp, no matter how genuine it may actually be, could never be passed off as *my* stamp. At best it would be accepted as a duplicate, a second Blue Error. More likely, philatelists would assume it was a fake, and he could never prove otherwise. He'd need my stamp for comparison – which, of course, he'd be unlikely to get. No reputable authority would bother trying to authenticate his stamp without mine beside it. This man understands all that."

"Sounds like it's worthless to him, then. Why are you willing to pay so much?"

Ollie sighed. "It's not worth the risk to call his bluff. Maybe he's got some kind of papers. Hell, even if he had forged papers, I'd have to go public to prove it. I can't take that chance. The safest thing to do is to buy the damn thing from him. It's insurance, part of the investment. I can afford it. Hell, I can't afford not to."

I sat back on the sofa. My cigar butt was cold, my brandy snifter empty. I patted my shirt pocket and extracted a Winston, lit it, and said, "And you'll pay his price. And the stamp-collecting world will be none the wiser. Right?"

Ollie smiled thinly. "Right Counselor."

"One question, then."

"Shoot."

"Why are you telling *me* all this?"

"Why, Brady. I'm surprised. You are my trusted attorney. You are bound by the ethic of absolute confidentiality. You are discreet. I *trust* you. And I pay you well for it."

"So?"

"So you will be my go-between?"

"Me? Hell, Ollie. Why me?"

"Who else?" Ollie thumped his withered thighs. "You have legs. You *can* go."

"But why . . .?"

"Ah. Why not Perry? Listen. He's my son, it's true. But he's also neither particularly bright nor particularly brave. You, having a generous endowment of both qualities, surely have observed that."

"Ah, he's not that bad."

"It's true. Listen. This transaction will be tricky. It needs a lawyer's mind. It needs an experienced hand. Not a boy."

"He's twenty-three years old."

"A boy. A baby."

"You don't do him justice, Ollie."

He smiled. "I don't trust him. Let's leave it at that, okay?"

I shrugged. "Okay. So what's next, then?"

"I have placed the notice in the

newspaper, as our friend has instructed. Now we wait. We'll do as he says. For a quarter of a million dollars cash money we'll buy the stamp and the man's commitment of secrecy."

"I have one question," I said.

"What is it?"

"How did this guy know you owned the stamp?"

Ollie stared at me.

"Perry?"

"Not Perry," he said firmly. "Perry knows that it wouldn't be in his interest. One thing Perry is smart about is his own interest."

"Then who?"

Ollie spread his hands. "I don't know. It's a piece of information that I would consider very valuable. If you follow me, Counselor."

I nodded. I followed him.

Chapter 2

Charlie McDevitt, one leg waving in the air, bent to inject the tee into the ground, leaning on his driver for balance. He looked like a big pastel heron in his mint-green and baby-pink golfing togs. He fit right into the orange and gold splendour of the late September woodlands that bordered the fairway.

"So this guy goes to his doctor for his annual physical," said Charlie, standing up to the ball and gazing down the fairway. "C'mon, ball. Right down the old pipe, now," he muttered. He cocked his right knee, pushed his hands forward a bit, then began his long, slow backswing. When he brought the driver forward, Charlie's hips jerked, his head snapped up, and his right foot left the ground in a graceless pirouette. He said "Umph!" as his club contacted the ball, and then "Ah, shit!" as it sliced toward the rough that lined the right of the fairway.

"Little Nicklaus fade, there," I said. "It'll play."

"Nuts," declared Charlie. "Banana ball. Anyhow, this guy sees his doctor and has the usual examination. EKG. Blood pressure. Rectal invasion. All the blood work, urine tests. Doctor listens to his ticker, takes his pulse, looks at his eyes and ears, pokes around in his mouth, fondles his private parts, raps his knees and wrists and heels with his little rubber mallet. Go ahead and hit."

"Okay," I said. Slow and easy, I told myself. It's all rhythm. Let the club do the work. I remembered all that right up until the last foot of the forward arc of the club, when the old baseball swing reasserted itself and my wrists flipped. The ball started out straight, a low line drive, before the hook took over, pulling the ball down and to the left. Into the pond.

"In the pond," said Charlie.

"I know."

"Tough break. That's a lateral water hazard. You can drop where it went in. Cost you a stroke."

"I know that, too."

"Hey, don't get snippy with me. I didn't hit your ball in the water." Charlie shouldered his bag. "Looks like you buy Cokes."

"I know, I know."

We started down the ninth fairway. "So, anyway," said Charlie, "after the exam is over the guy gets dressed and walks across the hall to the doctor's office. The doc's sitting behind his desk glancing through the guy's files, and the guy, he sits in the chair there, and the doctor says, 'Well, your blood pressure's fine, EKG perfectly normal, reflexes nice, your bowel and colon are clean as a clarinet, all the tests negative.' And the guy says, 'Good. That sounds real good.' And the doctor peers over his glasses and says to the guy, 'Look. I don't know how to tell you this, but, well, you've got this rare condition.' 'Rare condition?' says the guy. 'Yes,' says the doctor. 'You're gonna be dead by tomorrow. You better get yourself prepared.'"

Charlie headed over toward his ball, and I turned left toward the pond which had swallowed mine. I dropped a new ball over my right shoulder, then whacked a big four iron into the trap behind the green. Charlie caught some grass in the rough and dribbled up fifty yards short of the green.

"I've still got a chance," I told him as we met again in the fairway. "I get up and down in two, I've got my bogie. You've got to get par, or else we halve the hole and end up even for the nine. Meaning we buy our own Cokes."

"Watch me," said Charlie. He popped a

little wedge to within a foot and a half of the hole.

"I concede," I said. "Nice par."

I did not get up and down in two, anyway. We left our clubs by the tenth tee and walked back toward the clubhouse.

"So the guy goes home," continued Charlie, "and his wife says to him, 'So how was the exam? Everything okay?' And the guy says, 'Well, my heart's fine, blood pressure good, the whole GI nice and clean. All the tests were negative.' 'That's nice,' says his wife. 'Yeah,' says the guy, 'but the thing is, I'm gonna die sometime before tomorrow.' 'That's terrible,' says his wife. 'That's just awful. So how do you want to spend your last few hours?' 'Well,' the guy says, 'I've given it a lot of thought, and I decided what I really want to do is to spend the whole night with you making love.' And his wife looks at him and says, 'Easy for you to say. You don't have to get up in the morning.'"

I groaned as we pushed into the clubhouse. We went to the counter, I bought us our Cokes, and we took them to a table far from the television, which was showing a rerun of "Get Smart." Typical afternoon fare on the Boston UHF channels.

Tommy Porter, one of the owners of the

31

Green Acres Country Club, yelled from across the room, "Hey, Coyne. Call your office. Your, ah, secretary said it's urgent."

My "ah, secretary," as Tommy calls him, is a young law school graduate named Xerxes Garrett. Zerk, as he's called, is temporarily replacing my regular secretary, Julie, who's taking a six-month maternity leave. Zerk is handsome, bright, big and black, and studying, after a fashion, for the Massachusetts bar exam. He's got his pick of the classy old firms, and some day he'll make a million bucks if he decides he wants to. In the meantime, he says he's in no hurry to "get into the hassle," as he puts it. He answered my ad for a legal secretary and persuaded me, in a classic summation, that he was exactly what I was looking for.

He can make a typewriter sound like all the machine guns on the Western Front. "Quickest hands in Akron," he likes to boast, and although I somehow doubt he acquired that reputation from his secretarial skills, I have declined to ask.

"Why don't you get a beeper?" said Charlie. "All these important clients with all this emergency business."

"Aw, lay off, will you? It's part of my job, you know that."

"Yeah, bowing and scraping and tugging

your forelock to all those rich old crones. Somebody's chauffeur probably got a scratch on the El Dorado, huh?"

"Probably," I said. "Look, I'll be right back."

"I thought you were gonna argue civil liberties cases in front of the Supreme Court, and look at you," Charlie went on. "Can't even take a quiet Thursday afternoon on the links. Next thing you know, you'll be chasing ambulances."

"I thought I was going to be arguing civil liberties cases before you," I said.

"Touché," said Charlie, with a smart little salute. Charlie's law school dream had been to become a Supreme Court Justice. So far, he had made a career in the Justice Department's Boston office, prosecuting pension frauds and cocaine smugglers. "Difference is," he continued, "I'm on my way. Making contacts. Building bridges. I'll get there."

"And I won't," I finished for him. "You're probably right. Look, I gotta go to the phone."

The pay phone hung on the wall near the television. I punched in my credit card number, and a moment later Zerk said, "Brady L. Coyne, Attorney."

"At Law," I said. "You've gotta remember the At Law part."

"Brady L. Coyne, Attorney at the Golf Course," he said.

"So what is it, that you had to interrupt the superhuman concentration of the young Sam Snead?"

"Or is it the old Calvin Peete?" said Zerk.

"Calvin who?"

"Peete. Golf pro. Damn good one, too. Black. You probably never heard of him."

"Lots of people I never heard of, black, green, and purple," I said. "What's up?"

"Kentucky Fried Weston called."

"Don't be so goddam militant, Zerk. It sounds forced."

"Yassah, boss."

"What'd Ollie want?"

"To talk to you. I said you were unavailable. He said, 'Playing golf, eh?' I told him you were out on business, and he said, 'Playing golf with a client, then.' I told him you were conferring with someone from the Justice Department and he said he hoped you'd cured your hook. Have you?"

"Have I what?"

"Cured your hook?"

"No, for Christ's sake. Look, Zerk, we're gonna lose our place at the tenth tee if you don't tell me what Ollie wanted."

34

"I don't know. Wouldn't tell me. He just said for you to call him, that he got the call. Those were his words. 'Tell Brady I got the call, and for him to call me immediately.'"

"And you said?"

"I said I'd leave word at the clubhouse, but that you probably wouldn't get it until you finished your round."

"You know I always stop in for a Coke between nines."

"Sure. But I didn't tell him that."

"Good man. I'll call him when I'm done."

"I figured that's what you'd do."

Charlie was standing when I returned to our table. "We better hustle, we don't want to miss our place," he said. As we pushed out of the dark, air-conditioned cool of the clubhouse into the fall sunshine, Charlie said, "So what's the big emergency?"

"What do you know about philately?"

"Stamp collecting, right?"

"Not that much, huh? Well, did you know that the one-cent black and magenta British Guyana provisional of 1856 was bought at auction in the Waldorf-Astoria Hotel in New York City on April 5, 1980, for eight hundred and fifty thousand?"

"Funny how these important facts elude me," said Charlie. "So what about this black stamp?"

35

"Nothing about that one. Just that rare stamps are big business. Some of my clients are big businessmen. That's all."

"You're really into some heavy law, aren't you?" said Charlie as we arrived at the tenth tee.

"It's a living," I muttered. "It's your honor, Your Honor."

"He's going to call here again at nine tonight," said Ollie Weston when I called him from the clubhouse pay phone. "I want you to talk to him."

"Can't I call him?"

Ollie gave me that deep chuckle of his. "Hardly. He's very cautious. Wouldn't tell me anything – no name, no phone number, nothing. Just wanted to negotiate, and when I told him that you'd be doing my negotiating for me, he said he'd call again, and hung up on me. How'd you do, anyway?"

"How'd I do what?"

"Golf. How'd you hit?"

"Erratic. As usual. Okay. I'll be there by nine."

"Come earlier. Have a drink."

"Fine. Sometime around eight, then."

When I went back to where Charlie and I were having our beers, he had already ordered the second round. "Why don't you come out to the house and take potluck with us tonight?" he said. "Jenny keeps asking after you. She's worried you're not taking good care of yourself, since you and Gloria . . ."

"You can tell her I'm thriving on Big Macs and frozen pizza and Spaghetti-O's?"

"I tell her you're the envy of all us married guys and probably would hate to sit around the dining room table listening to the kids bicker and Jenny talk about her tennis pro and me complain about the bills."

"Well," I said, "you're wrong there. There's nothing I'd like better. But I've got an appointment tonight."

"Cancel it."

"Easy for you to say."

"Yeah, I know," said Charlie. "I don't have to get up in the morning."

Ollie Weston's big Victorian mansion in Belmont perches high on a hill, far back from the road. The twelve-foot iron fence, fully wired and tied directly into the Belmont Police Station, is screened by hemlocks and giant old rhododendrons. I entered the Weston estate through the tall iron gates, which swung silently open when I spoke into a telephone set in a box in one of the twin stone pillars. The long, peastone driveway terminated under a portico at the front door. I left my BMW beside the Weston Mercedes, climbed the steps onto the L-shaped front porch, and rang the bell. Off to my right, the lights of Cambridge and, beyond, Boston, blinked in the Indian summer dusk. I could distinguish the lights of my tall office building in Copley Square, flanked by the twin landmarks of the Pru and the Hancock Tower.

"Come right in, sir. Mr. Weston is expecting you."

"Jesus, Edwin. You startled me," I said to Ollie's man Friday, who has the disconcerting ability of gliding around as silently as if he were on ice skates, which I suppose is a trick of his trade.

I followed Edwin into the living room where the combination lock hid behind *The Road to Serfdom*. Standing by the bookshelves was Perry. We exchanged nods. Ollie was seated in a big, leather armchair. On the table in front of him stood a chess game waiting to be played. The black men were carved out of a green translucent stone which looked like jade. The other pieces were milky white. Probably some kind of marble. Or, knowing Ollie, rough-cut diamonds.

Another table stood by Ollie's right elbow,

where I saw a tray with three brandy snifters and a decanter two-thirds full of the amber liquid, and a black telephone. Ollie's wheelchair was nowhere in sight.

"Pull up a chair," greeted Ollie. "Your move."

I waved my hand. "No games tonight, Ollie. Offer me a drink, and let's talk about how we should handle this."

Ollie shrugged his thick shoulders. "Games are hard to avoid, my friend. Let's have some brandy, Perry."

Perry poured drinks for each of us and handed them around. Ollie lifted his glass up in front of his face and swirled the brandy gently, peering through it. Then he held the glass by the bowl, cupped in the palm of his hand, and stuck his long nose into it. He snuffled noisily and sighed. Only then did he sip. I could see his cheeks working as he rolled the liquor around in his mouth. Perry solemnly imitated his father's ritual, but I didn't. I sipped deeply from my glass and let the good brandy slide hotly down my throat.

"You, sir, are an unreconstructed peasant," said Ollie good-naturedly. "Fine brandy is wasted on you. Remind me to serve you Old Hipboot next time you come."

"Hey," I said. "Old Hipboot is good booze."

Ollie studied his glass for a moment. "Here's how we play it," he said, glancing briefly at Perry before settling his attention on me. "Tell me if this sounds okay. Our friend calls. I answer, tell him you're to handle the transaction, and give him right over to you. You set up a meeting. You must meet with him face to face. At that meeting you will first, verify that he *has* the stamp, and, second, arrange to have it authenticated. You will reassure him that I am quite serious about meeting his price. He may expect us to dicker. Don't. Authenticate the stamp, then buy it. Okay?"

"Sure. Sounds fine. How do we authenticate it, though?"

"Fellow by the name of Albert Dopplinger. He's an assistant curator at the Peabody Museum, specialist in paper and wood artifacts. Paintings and books, mostly. His lab has all the latest equipment. He knows all about inks, paints, the manufacture of paper, and so forth. He's done some work for me personally. I've already talked to him. He says he'll have no problem authenticating the stamp. He's acknowledged among philatelists as one of the preeminent experts in the area of old stamps, though he isn't a philatelist himself. He's got no interest in collecting things. Just likes to examine them.

Which suits me fine. The last person I want involved in this is some philatelic dealer or agent. This Dopplinger, I think, we can trust to remain discreet. We'll pay him well. And he knows he can count on a tidy little sidelight moonlighting for me."

"That sounds easy enough," I said. "What else?"

"Well, there is one little problem," said Ollie. He sipped his brandy. I waited for him to continue.

"You sure you won't play chess?" he said after a moment. "Most instructive game."

"C'mon, Ollie. What's the problem?"

"The problem is this. Dopplinger says that in order for him to authenticate the duplicate Dutch Blue Error he'll need to have the original for comparison. You'll have to bring my stamp with you. You appreciate what that means, don't you?"

I lifted my eyebrows. "It means," I said, "that I'll be carrying the equivalent of a million dollars in cash."

"Or close to it. Yes. Of course, the stamp without the papers isn't worth that much, and those I'll keep in my vault. Still, if that stamp gets into the wrong hands . . ."

"It'll cost you a fortune to get it back. I understand. That's a heavy responsibility, Ollie."

"I pay you heavy fees. Are you licensed?"

"Huh?"

"Licensed. To carry."

Perry, who had remained standing, and who appeared not to be paying any attention to our discussion, suddenly blurted, "Oh, Jesus Christ!"

I glanced at Perry, then at Ollie. "Oh. You mean a gun. Sure. But do you think . . .?"

"Absolutely. You carry my stamp, you carry a gun. And make sure our friend knows you have it."

Perry rolled his eyes. I shrugged, then nodded. We sat back to wait for the phone to ring. Perry pretended to study the rows of books. I fired up a Winston. Ollie cradled his nearly empty brandy glass in both of his hands on his stomach as he slouched in his big chair. His eyes were closed. He looked very old. His skin had taken on that transparent, waxy cast of the terminally ill. Ollie Weston, with his eyes closed and his hands folded across his stomach, looked like a corpse.

"Get his name," Ollie said suddenly, his eyes still closed.

"Huh?"

When he calls. Get his name, if you can. I'd like to check up on him."

"Okay." I glanced at my watch. It read

42

8:58. I looked at the telephone, willing it to ring. When it did, precisely two minutes later, I jumped as if I had been stabbed.

Ollie picked up the receiver after the third ring, said "Yes?", listened a moment, then said, "I'm putting you on to Mr. Coyne, my attorney." Then he handed the phone to me.

"This is Brady Coyne," I said. "With whom am I speaking?"

"Never mind that, Mr. Coyne. Are you prepared to do business with me?"

"Not over the phone I'm not. Would you please identify yourself?"

"Not yet." The man's voice was devoid of inflection, as near as I could tell. It was deep, well modulated, and sounded cultivated. An educated person, I thought, and an older man, nearer Ollie's age than mine. "You want to meet me, then," he continued. "All right. Listen carefully. Tomorrow afternoon at three. Do you know the Wursthaus?"

"In Harvard Square. Yes, I know it."

"Awful food, I'm sure you'll agree. Take a booth by yourself. Order a bottle of Beck's. Put a briefcase on the table. Wear a red necktie. I'll find you."

"Three o'clock at the Wursthaus. Bottle of Beck's, briefcase on the table, red necktie.

43

Okay," I said. "Now, may I please know who this is?"

"In due time, Mr. Coyne," the voice answered. "And I trust you're not planning anything fancy."

"Fancy?"

"I intend to be very cautious about this, you see. I hold all the cards, don't you agree?"

"Look, mister. I'm an attorney. I'm helping my client consummate a business deal. That's all. Mr. Weston is an upstanding and honorable . . ."

"When there's a quarter-million dollars at stake, nobody's upstanding or honorable," he interrupted. "Tomorrow at three, then."

"How will I recognize you?"

"When I sit down with you, that will be me. If I turn out to be a lady, it's not me."

"May I please have your name?"

"See you at the Wursthaus." There was a click at the other end of the line.

Ollie was staring at me as I hung up the phone. "So what's his name?"

"He wouldn't give it to me."

"Jesus, Brady. The one thing I ask you to do is get his name. You should have gotten his name.

44

"Easy for you to say," I said. "You don't have to get up in the morning."

Ollie said he didn't get it. Perry, leaning back against the bookshelves, smiled as if he did.

Chapter 3

I took the subway to Cambridge from my office, because I knew I'd never find a parking space in the Square. On the other hand, the ride on the T was no pleasure, either. I vowed that I'd either walk all the way back, or at least walk to my office from the Park Street stop. Boston's subway lines aren't really laid out the way the roads are, following the old cow paths from Colonial days. It just seems that way. There is some logic to the relationships among the Green Line and the Orange Line and Park Street Under and the North Station. It just eludes me. I go to New York three or four times a year and have no problem navigating the Manhattan underground. I've lived in Boston my whole life, and I still carry a knot of anxiety in my stomach every time I descend into my city's subterranean labyrinth.

Zerk tells me that it's a racist thing. Maybe he's right. The black kids race through the cars at night in groups of five or six. More often than not, they don't bother to assault, rob, rape, or stab anybody. On the other hand, sometimes they do. During rush hour I experience what claustrophobics must feel in an elevator. I begin to sweat, my hands tremble, and my knees turn to chocolate mousse. I always keep one hand in my hip pocket to guard my wallet while I stand in the overcrowded cars, propped up by sweaty people on all sides of me.

Harvard Square seems downright respectable to me nowadays. Fewer glassy-eyed girls with scratched faces and dirty bare feet loiter on the sidewalks asking for handouts, fewer Bill Russell-sized dudes in African garb and grand, curly helmets slouch around trying to look militant. There's more of a mix of secretaries, businessmen, professional types, students, and out-of-towners bustling around in front of the Coop and along Mt. Auburn Street, in and out of the bookstores and the tall, glass-fronted shops that sell colorful fabrics and Scandinavian furniture.

Perhaps I don't go there at the right times of day – or night – but it seems that most of the people I see in Harvard Square are a lot like me.

I had to wait a few minutes before a booth opened up at the Wursthaus. I slid into it, hoisted my briefcase (which I don't carry with me normally) onto the table, and

47

ordered a Beck's from the fat waitress. I wore a solid red tie which I found in the back of my closet. I hadn't worn it for several years, since the time at a party when a girl who was telling me about meeting Red Auerbach at Joyce Chen's interrupted herself to observe that my tie looked like my tongue hanging down to lap my own penis. I laughed at the time, complimented the girl on her vivid imagination, and relegated the necktie to the back of my closet.

"You're Mr. Coyne?"

He had managed to slide into the booth across from me almost before I noticed him. It was as if he had materialized there. I glanced at my watch. The digital readout said precisely 3:00 p.m. This guy was prompt. He'd make the trains run.

"Let's see," I said. "Briefcase. Beck's. Ugly red tie. I must be Coyne."

He didn't offer a smile, nor did he extend either his hand or his name to me. A shock of thin, white hair fell over his forehead. His red scalp gleamed through it. A great, purple rutabaga of a nose was heaved up out of the red, furrowed clay of his face. Small, blue eyes glittered out of the florid puffiness of his flesh. Late sixties, overweight, alcohol problem. A Boston Irishman, I guessed. Southie High, B.A. in Business Administration at B.C. to account for the veneer of cultured speech I had noticed on the telephone. Flynn, Shea, Callahan, O'Leary. Mother waitressed at Durgin Park to put him through school. Old man a motorman on the MBTA. I thought I knew the type. Now where the hell would a guy like this get a rare postage stamp worth a quarter-million dollars?

"You ready to do business, Mr. Coyne?"

"I don't even know your name," I said. "Perhaps now that we've met face-to-face, you could introduce yourself."

His broad smile revealed excellent teeth. Too excellent. An expensive set of dentures, uppers and lowers. "Of course," he said, reaching his hand across the table. "Daniel F. X. Sullivan, at your service."

I took his hand. "Pleasure, Mr. Sullivan." I didn't bother telling him that I didn't believe we were using his real name. For now, I couldn't see that it mattered. "Yes, I'm prepared to do business," I continued. "My client doesn't wish to haggle with you. He considers your price reasonable, provided the item is what you claim it to be."

Sullivan, or whatever his name really was, bowed his head. "Mr. Weston is a wise man. Haggling would prove counterproductive to him. I assure you, Mr. Coyne, the item is genuine."

"Regardless, I'm sure you understand that he wishes to take no chances in that regard. I have arranged to have your item, authenticated. Unless, of course, you can provide documents . . ."

"I have no documents. I told you, no one knows that I possess this stamp. That, as we both know, is what makes it valuable to Mr. Weston. The stamp was discovered. Its value was unsuspected until it came into my hands. I have told nobody about it, except Mr. Weston."

"That was shrewd," I said. "You must know a lot about the world of rare stamps, Mr. Sullivan, to go straight to the man who owns the only other copy of the Dutch Blue Error."

Sullivan dipped his head, as if in modest embarrassment, but said nothing.

"Are you willing to permit us to authenticate your stamp?" I persisted.

"I assumed you'd want to. What's the arrangement? Can you assure me that my interests will be protected?"

"We have no desire to do anything except purchase the stamp, Mr. Sullivan. Your protection, it seems to me, is your knowledge. And our knowledge of it."

Sullivan showed his dentures again. "Precisely. I'm glad you understand that."

"If you will meet me in front of the main entrance to the Peabody Museum tomorrow afternoon at this same time – three o'clock – we have an appointment with a curator there. Mr. Weston trusts his expertise. Assuming he authenticates the stamp, we will then arrange the actual transaction. Fair enough?"

"That sounds fair. I'll be there at three."

"With the stamp."

"Of course."

Sullivan began to push himself out of the booth. "One moment, Mr. Sullivan," I said. "You haven't even had a beer. Won't you have a drink with me?"

He held up his hand. "Doctor's orders, Mr. Coyne."

"I did want to ask you one thing."

Sullivan stood beside the table, looking down at me. "And what was that?"

"Mr. Weston is most eager to know how you learned that he owned the Blue Error."

Sullivan eased himself back into the booth, placed both elbows on the table, and leaned his face toward mine. "I'm sure he is, Mr. Coyne. I have no doubt that he would like very much to know how I learned that. But I'm really surprised at you."

"How's that?"

"Why, how I learned Mr. Weston's secret is my protection. I'm sure Mr. Weston appreciates just how well protected that knowledge makes me. I'm equally certain that you, Mr. Coyne, do *not* appreciate the value of what I know. In case there is any doubt, please be sure to convey this message to your employer."

"He's my client, not my employer."

"Whatever," said Sullivan, with a wave of his hand. "Tell Mr. Weston this: Not only do I know *that* he owns the Dutch Blue Error, but I also know *how* he came into possession of it, and I know about *all* the precautions he has taken to protect his secret. Be sure to tell him that, Mr. Coyne. And I'm sure he will instruct you to be most solicitous of my interests in this matter. Okay?"

"I'll tell him," I said with a shrug. "Three tomorrow, then."

"I'll be there," said Daniel F. X. Sullivan, and with a half-wave he disappeared.

My appointment at the Peabody Museum with Sullivan had been set for Saturday afternoon. Albert Dopplinger, the assistant curator, did not usually work on Saturdays, so he was free to carry on some free-lance business. The museum, I was given to understand by Ollie Weston, allowed Dopplinger to use his laboratory on his own time.

Sullivan, we figured, would have to know that authentication of his stamp would require us to bring Ollie's original. Using the museum at its busiest time of the week – a Saturday afternoon – would protect us all. Neither of us could easily do violence to the other with hundreds of people wandering all over the big building.

I asked Zerk to meet me at the office at noon. I wanted him with me. Zerk had gone both ways as linebacker and fullback at Tufts as an undergraduate. He remained a sturdy fellow. I knew I'd feel more comfortable if I had the quickest hands in Akron along with me.

Zerk walked in as I was bent over the safe in my conference room. When I straightened up, he said, "Now what the hell do you want *that* thing for? I thought we were going to take a tour of the stuffed birds and Egyptian mummies."

I spun the cylinder of my .38-caliber Smith and Wesson in what I knew was a poor imitation of Kojak, snapped it into place, and tucked the heavy weapon into my jacket pocket. "You never can tell," I said out of the corner of my mouth. "Could be some foul play."

"Foul play!" screeched Zerk, his face collapsing in laughter. "Holy shit, man. Foul play! Hey, can you handle that thing?"

I jerked a Winston out of the pack on my desk and shoved it into the corner of my mouth. "Better believe it, baby."

Zerk put his hands over his ears and slowly shook his head. Then he said, "Seriously. If you'll pretend you're a forty-something-year-old Boston attorney, I'll play the eager, young law school graduate. We'll leave the weapon in your safe here, and everyone will know exactly where they stand. Okay?"

"I'm bringing the gun, Zerk. Don't worry, I have no intention of using it. Ollie Weston thought it would be a good idea."

"Ollie Weston! That guy thinks he's Papa Hemingway still playing with bad guys on the frontier. That's no way to do business. Believe me. I know about that stuff. You don't want to be carrying a weapon."

I shrugged. "My choice. You ready to go?"

Zerk threw his hands into the air. "You're the boss."

When we pulled up under the portico in front of the Weston estate, Zerk, who was driving, said, "I'll just wait right here."

"You should meet Ollie Weston. He's a good man to know."

Zerk held up his hands. "I'll pass. Places like this, people like him – they make me nervous. I can't help it. It's my heritage. My roots."

"Bugger your roots," I said. "Whatever happened to upward mobility?"

He shook his head. "I'll wait here."

Ollie was out in the back garden sitting in his wheelchair reading *Field & Stream*. He wore a ratty brown sweater against the autumn chill. Edwin offered me coffee and de-materialized when I declined. When I sat down beside him, Ollie reached inside his jacket and pulled out the pigskin volume. "Here you go," he said.

I accepted the Dutch Blue Error in both of my hands.

"You're armed?"

"Yes, I feel silly, but I'm armed."

"You'll remember to arrange the transaction for the middle of next week. It'll take me a few days to round up the cash."

"You're giving him cash?"

"Perhaps I should write him a personal check? Suppose our friend will take American Express?"

"Yeah, right," I said. "Assuming his stamp is genuine, of course."

"Of course," Ollie grinned. "Go, now. I doubt that our Mr. Sullivan would like it if you were late. I don't want any foul-ups."

"Right." I turned to go.

"Brady."

I stopped. "Yes?"

"Take care, will you?"

"No sweat, Ollie."

Zerk and I drove the short distance from Ollie's house in Belmont to the Peabody Museum in Cambridge in silence. I was disappointed that he refused to allow me to introduce him to Ollie Weston. He, I knew, disapproved of my choice of clients. We would have to talk through this little value conflict between us. I knew I'd have to take the first step, because I understood his position. I had entered law school so that I could right the world's wrongs, too. The difference was, my commitment was arbitrary, and shallow, and readily adjusted to the conditions of my life. When I got my degree at Yale Law I was a young, inexperienced attorney who had but a single ambition: I wanted to go it alone. So I took the clients who wanted me. The first one was a rich old lady with a son missing in the Vietnam War. She recommended me to her friends, also wealthy. And so it went. I found that wealthy people like to retain discreet attorneys, just to handle whatever might come up. I discovered wealthy people paid generously for discretion. I discovered I could live quite comfortably serving wealthy people. Anyway, justice, as they keep telling us, is blind. Everyone has an equal right to legal protection, rich and poor. I happen to have ended up with the rich.

And if that sounds like an apology, I suppose it is.

Zerk's commitment, of course, went deeper than mine. I had no desire to change it. I simply wanted him to respect our difference. So far I had done a poor job of it.

Zerk found a parking space on the street a couple of blocks from the Peabody Museum. We got to the front entrance with ten minutes to spare. We sat on the steps in the dim September sunlight to wait for our friend, Daniel F. X. Sullivan.

The Peabody Museum is an example of the functional school of architecture. It's big, bulky, square, and gray – unmistakably a museum. The rooms inside are abundant, and large enough to contain reconstructed dinosaurs and whales, stuffed animals, and birds of every conceivable size and shape, as well as glass flowers. I'm convinced that you could spend months there without examining the same exhibit twice or dallying too long at any one of them. Inside, it smells vaguely of formaldehyde and dust. The floors are dark, scarred wood, the walls dirty white plaster. My boys, when they were younger, never tired of spending Saturdays wandering among the exhibits at the Peabody. They would come home chattering endlessly about the snakes and the mummies, and end up having bad dreams.

When that happened after our divorce, Gloria was able to transform even a well-intentioned visit to a museum into a guilt trap for the once-a-week father. Gloria was an expert at that sort of thing.

"You must be Brady Coyne," said a voice beside us.

I looked up from where I sat on the museum steps. Peering down at us was a smiling, bespectacled young man with a curved, banana-shaped nose more or less bisecting his face. He reached down with his hand. "Am I right? Albert Dopplinger."

I took his hand as I stood up. "You're right. Nice to meet you. This is my associate, Xerxes Garrett."

Zerk rose and shook Dopplinger's hand. I noticed that the young curator stood several inches taller than Zerk, which is going some. Zerk is six-two. On the other hand, I guessed

58

that Zerk, who went about two-twenty, had at least fifty pounds on young Dopplinger.

"How'd you recognize me?" I asked him.

"Ah, details, Mr. Coyne. My stock in trade. You fit the general description, of course. Fortyish, but well-preserved. Touch of gray at the temples. A shade over six feet. No rings on your fingers. No shine on your shoes. And the scar that interrupts your left eyebrow. Who else could you be?"

"Ollie described me that way, eh? Even the part about the shoes.?"

"The shoes and the scar were the important details, Mr. Coyne. Well. Is the other party here yet?"

I glanced at my watch. "He'll arrive in precisely three minutes, unless I miss my guess. Will this take long?"

"It shouldn't. If you have the original stamp, it's simply a matter of comparison. The grain of the paper, age of the ink, watermarks, cancellations, that sort of thing. We so-called experts like to preserve the aura of mystery about our science, but really there's not much to it. I guarantee you, if this fellow's stamp is a fake, I'll spot it. I'll stake my reputation on it."

"You're staking several of Ollie Weston's dollars on it, Mr. Dopplinger."

"Albert, please. Okay? And Brady, is it? And . . ." He looked at Zerk.

"Mr. Garrett," said Zerk.

Dopplinger looked confused for a moment, then he shrugged. "Sure, okay. Mr. Garrett."

"Are we all here now?" A hand touched my arm. I whirled around to face Daniel F. X. Sullivan. His hand had brushed my jacket pocket where my Smith and Wesson .38 sagged uncomfortably.

I introduced Sullivan to Dopplinger and Zerk, and the four of us climbed the broad steps and entered the museum. Dopplinger led the way. We turned right, through a room lined with glass cases containing Indian artifacts. There were hundreds of pieces of stone. Some of them were recognizably arrowheads, hatchets, spear points, and hand tools. Most of them appeared to be no more than randomly shaped bits of obsidian and flint. Some exhibits contained shards of pottery – uniformly dull gray or brown. When we left the Indian room we turned sharp left, descended a steep stairway, turned again, followed a long, dimly lit corridor lined with closed wooden doors without windows, and went down another stairway. We had entered the bowels of the Peabody Museum. At the bottom of this stairway,

Dopplinger pushed through a pair of swinging doors, turned left, and stopped outside a door that might have opened into a broom closet. He fished a key from his pants pocket, inserted it into the lock, and pushed open the door for us.

"Be it ever so humble," he said, ushering us in with a little bow.

Dopplinger's laboratory was long and narrow and windowless. From its high ceilings hung two long rows of fluorescent bulbs which flickered on sequentially as the scientist threw the switches by the door. A narrow, waist-high island bisected the length of the room. It was equipped with sinks, gas jets, microscopes, and goose-neck lamps. Along the far wall stood glass cabinets crammed with jars and boxes and equipment.

"Make yourself at home," said Dopplinger. He plucked a green apron from a hook, replaced the glasses he had been wearing with another pair from his shirt pocket, and bustled around the room. From the cabinets, he took down three jars containing liquid chemicals. He placed these beside a microscope. Sullivan and Zerk and I each perched on a high stool. We watched Dopplinger prepare himself. I felt wary, cautious, awkward. I could sense Zerk's tension. Sullivan appeared to be thoroughly at ease.

I spoke in a low voice to Sullivan, so that Dopplinger wouldn't hear me but Zerk might. "I want you to know, Mr. Sullivan, that I am carrying a revolver. It is in my pocket where my hand is. It is pointed at you. Just to insure that all of this goes smoothly, you understand."

Sullivan turned his head slowly to smile at me. "That's just fine," he said quietly. "Of course I understand. And by the way, the little twenty-two automatic in *my* pocket is presently directed towards the kidneys of your young colored friend there. I, too, am committed to the proposition that this transaction be consummated without undue disturbance. So we seem to be at a stalemate of sorts, Mr. Coyne."

"So we do," I said. I kept my hand in my pocket. If Zerk heard Sullivan's use of the word "colored," he gave no indication of it.

"There. I guess we're about all set." Albert Dopplinger had climbed atop a stool and was twisting his fingers into a pair of surgical rubber gloves. Then he extracted a small notebook from his hip pocket and placed it beside him. "If I can have the stamps, gentlemen, this shouldn't take but a few minutes."

I looked at Sullivan, who returned my stare for a moment, then shrugged and reached into the inside pocket of his sports jacket. He removed a thin cardboard folder, which he handed to the curator. Dopplinger placed it directly before him on the table and gingerly opened the cover. Inside, tucked into a slot, was a glassine envelope. Dopplinger removed the envelope from the cardboard folder, lifted the flap, and reached inside with tweezers to remove the tiny blue square of paper. He placed the stamp in a shallow black ceramic tray. Then he looked at me.

"Mr. Coyne? I'll need your stamp, too."

"Sure," I said, and handed him the pigskin album. Dopplinger removed Ollie Weston's Dutch Blue Error with his tweezers and arranged it beside Sullivan's under a very bright white light.

Dopplinger then bent his face so close to the two stamps that his big nose nearly touched them. He muttered "Hm" and "Ah, yes." He seemed to have forgotten that the rest of us were present. Sullivan and Zerk and I hitched our stools closer.

Dopplinger set a beaker of water on a tripod over a Bunsen burner, and when the water was boiling briskly he picked up Sullivan's stamp with the tweezers and dunked it. He held it there for a moment, grunted, then removed the bit of blue paper and laid it on a piece of paper towel. Then he scratched a few lines into his notebook.

"Tell us what you're doing," said Zerk.

"Sh!" said Dopplinger.

With an eye dropper, he extracted some clear liquid from one of the glass jars and dabbed the stamp. Then he again bent close to it. After a moment, he lifted the stamp with the tweezers and placed it on a glass slide under a big microscope. He adjusted the lens and peered through it, humming tunelessly in the back of his throat. Then he repeated the process with the other stamp – Ollie's. I watched him carefully, as if he were a carnival sharpie with a pea under walnut shells. I wanted to be sure the two stamps did not become confused.

Dopplinger shifted his attention to the notebook which lay open by his elbow. He scribbled into it for a moment. Then he repeated the previous process, this time with a different chemical. Again he made some notes. Then he fiddled with the microscope, peered through it, and turned more knobs. Evidently satisfied, he placed both stamps side by side under the lens. With the tweezers, he pushed them together so that their edges were touching. He stared at them through the lens, muttered "Humph!" and reversed the position of the two stamps. This time when he looked he said quite clearly, "Just as I thought." He wrote in his notebook for a minute, then closed it and shoved it back into his pocket.

He straightened up slowly and spun around on the stool to face us. He lifted his glasses off his ears, using both hands. Carefully he folded them, returned them to his shirt pocket, and reached up to pinch the bridge of his nose. Then he put his other glasses back on.

"Well?" said Zerk.

"Oh, it's genuine, all right," said Dopplinger. "They're both genuine. Matter of fact, they were originally paired."

"Paired?" repeated Sullivan.

"Yes. Attached. These stamps – they have no perforations, like most stamps today. Those little holes along the edges to make tearing them apart easy. They just came in a sheet, and you had to cut them apart with scissors. These two stamps were once next to each other on the sheet. Here, look."

Dopplinger laid the two stamps side by side on the black enamel tray. All three of us crowded together to look over his shoulder. He pushed the two stamps together. They did seem to fit nicely, although to my eye it was simply a matter of two straight edges naturally matching up. I kept my opinion to myself.

"The other thing," continued Dopplinger, "is the water-mark. Both copies of the stamp have the same watermark. It's very faint. I can only bring it out with the carbon tet, but it looks like this." He tore a piece of paper from a pad on the table and drew what looked like a powderhorn hanging by a thong. "This is in the paper on both stamps. Actually, your stamp," he said, turning to Sullivan, "is in somewhat better condition than Mr. Weston's. The postmark is a shade lighter, and Mr. Weston's stamp has a thin spot in the upper left corner. A fine copy, still, but not quite as good as this other one."

Dopplinger returned Ollie's stamp to its plastic pouch inside the pigskin album and handed it to me. He tweezed Sullivan's into the glassine envelope, stuck it back inside the cardboard folder, and held it for Sullivan to take. Albert Dopplinger had not mixed the two stamps up.

"You seem to know your stuff, all right," said Sullivan with a broad smile, tucking the folder back into his jacket pocket. He turned to me. "Satisfied, Mr. Coyne?"

"Yes, I am," I answered. "I'll have to

report this to Mr. Weston, of course, but I think we can safely plan our transaction."

"I'll draw up the papers of authentication and mail them to Mr. Weston," said Dopplinger.

"No copies," I told him, remembering Ollie's instructions. "And be sure to include your notes. Mr. Weston must have everything that has been written."

Dopplinger smiled, his mouth curving up on either side of his pendulous nose. "Of course. I've done business with Mr. Weston before. I value the work he gives me. And now, gentlemen, if you'll excuse me, I have a manuscript which is purported to be J. S. Bach's rough notes for his Third Brandenburg Concerto . . ."

"Oh, sure," said Sullivan. "Just one thing, though."

"Yes?" said Dopplinger.

"How the hell do we get out of here?"

"I know," said Zerk. "Follow me."

We all shook hands with the tall curator and walked out of his laboratory. Zerk led the way. Sullivan stayed behind me. I could sense his .22 automatic pointing at my spine. I was glad Zerk was with me.

The chill afternoon breeze outside the museum made me shiver. The three of us stood on the sidewalk. I held out my hand to Sullivan. He gave me a little embarrassed smile, then withdrew his hand, which had been caressing his weapon, from his jacket pocket.

"So how shall we do it?" he asked, grasping my hand quickly.

"Let's see," I said, pretending to be thinking about it for the first time. Why don't I give you a call – hm, today's Saturday – oh, say, next Tuesday?"

"I'll call you," he said firmly. "Will you have the cash by then?"

"Cash. Yes, I suppose so," I said. "Okay. Call me at my office at noon on Tuesday, and we'll arrange the exchange."

I took a business card from my wallet and handed it to him. "I'm in the phone book, if you lose it," I added.

"I won't lose it, Mr. Coyne. I'm a very careful man."

"Yes. I imagine you are."

"I'll call you at noon on Tuesday, then. You'll have two hundred and fifty thousand dollars in cash – nothing larger than five hundreds, please. I'll have the stamp."

He turned abruptly and walked away.

"Let's go get a drink," said Zerk.

"In a minute. Do you think you can find Dopplinger's lab again?"

"Sure. We coloreds have an uncanny sense of direction. It's in our blood, you know."

"Right. Along with your innate rhythm and athletic ability. Comes from your ancestors creeping through the trackless jungle of Africa. You caught it, then."

"Sure. I caught it. 'Colored friend!' Shee-it! If that honkie wasn't someone we had to do business with . . ."

"He had a gun, you know."

"Sure I knew it. Knew it the minute I saw him. You can't carry a gun in your pocket without it showing."

"I guess you develop an eye for that sort of thing," I said.

"It's in the blood."

"You could tell I had one, too?"

Zerk laughed. "It was as plain as the nose on Dopplinger's face."

"Take me to him, okay?"

Dopplinger's door was locked, and he took several minutes to open it when I knocked. "Oh. You," he said when he saw us. "What is it? I'm right in the middle of something."

"Sorry to bother you. There's one more thing you'll have to do to complete your part in all this. Mr. Weston insists that you be present when the stamp exchanges hands. That will probably be Tuesday afternoon,

69

but if that's not convenient for you, I need to know."

"Where will this deal take place?"

"There's a lounge on the top floor of the Hyatt Regency on Memorial Drive. Called The Spinnaker. Know it?"

"The floor revolves so you can see the whole three-sixty degrees of the city. Sure, I know it. Damn near got seasick there once." Dopplinger consulted his little notebook. "I can be there at five-thirty, if that's all right."

"Fine. You understand . . ."

"Sure I understand. Can't have your friend pulling the old switcheroo. You'll want me to verify that the stamp you buy is the same one I examined today. That will be simple. Magnifying glass is all I'll need. No problem."

"Good. Thanks. Unless you hear otherwise, we'll see you then." I shook Dopplinger's hand again, and Zerk escorted me out of the museum's maze for the second time.

As he drove us back into the city, Zerk said, "Suppose he's planning to rob you. A man'll do a lot for a quarter-million, cash money."

"I'm not too worried."

"No? Why not?"

"I'll have you with me."

"Ah," said Zerk. "That explains it."

Chapter 4

Tuesday morning, 11:47 A.M. by my wristwatch. I pressed the button on my console.

"Yup?" came Zerk's amplified voice.

"How about a cup of coffee?"

"Black, right?"

"If you'll excuse the expression."

A minute later Zerk entered my inner office bearing the stained and chipped coffee mug that my son Joey constructed for me in his ninth-grade pottery class. He put it on the desk at my elbow and said, "Can I ask you something?"

"Sure. That's why you're here. To learn."

"Okay. Here's my question. Did Julie used to bring you coffee when you buzzed her?"

I sipped from my mug. "You've got to understand," I said, "that Julie – well, she thought that was, ah, demeaning to a woman. I mean, at first she did – bring me coffee, do some shopping for me, like that. Then one day she told me she wouldn't any more. That it wasn't her job, wasn't what she was trained to do, wasn't what I hired her for and paid her good money for. So after that we brought each other coffee."

Zerk nodded. "That's what I figured."

"Aha."

"Yeah," he said. "Aha. It's bad enough I have to sit there by the typewriter and the telephone and greet the rich white folks who walk through the door, smile and make them feel right at home when they're staring at me. But bringing you coffee, man . . ."

"Sure, I get it. Something else to do with your heritage, right? The old roots again."

"No more coffee, okay?"

"Okay," I shrugged. "That's fair enough, I guess. But greeting the clients, answering the phone, typing the letters – that's the job. You're a secretary here, remember, not a lawyer. I didn't ask to have a black man for this position, you may recall. I expected something with slimmer legs, actually. Something of the female persuasion is what I had in mind. You asked for this job, remember?"

"Yeah, I remember. But I didn't expect I was going to be treated like a . . ."

"Like a woman."

He glared at me. "Okay. Like a woman."

I cocked an eyebrow at him. "How should a woman be treated then?"

He stared at me for a moment, then his face burst into a broad grin. "Okay. You got me. Still, no coffee, right?"

I nodded. "Right. Listen. Sullivan is going to call in a couple minutes. Any other calls between now and then, tell them I'll get right back to them. I don't think I want to keep our Mr. Sullivan waiting."

"Gotcha," said Zerk, and returned to his desk in the reception area.

When my watch said 11:59, I lit a Winston, sipped the last of my coffee, and hitched myself up to my desk. I watched the buttons on my phone console, waiting for one of them to begin blinking.

Noon came and went. At ten after twelve I walked out to the outer office, where Zerk was doing a good Gene Krupa imitation on his typewriter.

"No calls, huh?" I said.

"Not yet," he answered, without missing a beat on his IBM.

"That's odd. He's been compulsively prompt up to now. Our lines haven't been tied up, have they?"

Zerk removed his hands from the typewriter, folded them under his chin, and twisted his head around to look up at me.

"You want me to get out this letter, or you want to make idle conversation? Our man

74

hasn't called. When he does, I'll let you know. Okay?"

I shrugged. "Sure. Okay. Sorry." I returned to my desk.

At twelve-thirty Zerk brought in some letters for me to sign. "No call," he said.

At one o'clock I tried to smooth out a couple of clauses in a complicated will I was working on. I kept glancing at the row of unlit buttons on my console, and at my watch, and back at the phone.

At quarter to two I went out and said to Zerk, "Look, ordinarily I wouldn't mention it, but I really don't want to leave the phones and I haven't had a bite since my untoasted English muffin and peanut butter at six-thirty this morning..."

He nodded. "No sweat. What do you want?"

"Tuna salad on rye. Chocolate shake. And Zerk?"

"Yeah?"

"Thanks. This isn't part of your job description."

"I know. That's why I'm doing it."

At four, Zerk and I were sitting across from each other on the twin sofas in the conference area in my office. I was tossing out hypothetical questions of law to him, and he was citing cases and precedents. Part of the deal we made when he persuaded me to hire him.

"Ballinger v. Moorehouse, 1963," he said. "Prior restraint not applicable. He's not gonna call."

"What?"

"Sullivan. He's not going to call. He chickened out."

"Why would a man who's about to earn a quarter-million dollars in smallish bills chicken out?"

"He was going to rob you. His henchmen backed out."

"His henchmen. Jesus Christ! Nah, I don't buy that."

"Well," said Zerk, "maybe his car broke down. His telephone's out of order, and he's got to wait for the repairman. He got a broken leg. His wife made him mow the lawn. Lots of things could have happened. So he'll call tomorrow."

I sighed. "Maybe. Somehow it doesn't fit, though. Well, there's nothing we can do. Look. Will you call the Peabody Museum and tell Dopplinger he doesn't have to meet us at The Spinnaker? Hate for him to make the trip for nothing. Save him a case of *mal de mer*."

"Sure." Zerk returned to his desk.

A moment later he buzzed me. "He's left already. Now what?"

"I don't know. Call The Spinnaker and leave him a message, I guess. Best we can do. Oh, well. I better call Ollie."

I rang the Weston number in Belmont. "The Weston residence," answered Edwin.

"This is Brady Coyne. Let me speak to Mr. Weston, please."

"I'm afraid Mr. Weston can't come to the phone, Mr. Coyne. May I take a message?"

I thought for a moment. "Tell him the transaction has been delayed," I said. "Is Ollie all right?"

"Excuse me, Mr. Coyne. Master Weston would like a word with you."

"Perry? Okay, then."

A moment later I heard Perry's voice. "Brady? How'd it go? Have you got the stamp?"

"What's wrong with Ollie?"

"They don't exactly know. The spinal thing, you know, it's progressive. He's been having a lot of pain. I mean, when my father complains about pain, you know he's feeling it. Anyhow, the doctor was here. Wanted to hospitalize him. Fat chance of that. He did allow himself to be put to bed and sedated, which the doctor seemed to consider a medical breakthrough worthy of an article

77

in the *New England Journal of Medicine*. I'm sure there'll be a headline in the *Globe* tomorrow. 'Financial Wizard Admits Pain,' it'll say. Subhead: 'Weston Takes a Pill.' So, anyhow, did you get it?"

"No."

There was a pause. "No?"

"No. The deal didn't happen. Sullivan never called. I've still got Ollie's money in my office safe."

Perry said, "Hm."

"So tell Ollie that for me, will you? Tell him I'll fill him in later. When he's able to talk. We'll decide what to do next."

Perry was silent for a moment. "You can talk to me, you know."

"I know, Perry."

"I mean, God damn it, I'm not a kid."

"I didn't mean anything. Sure, we can talk about it."

"He might not get better, you know."

"Well, I hope he does."

"How do you figure it, anyway? Sullivan not calling."

"I don't. It makes no sense."

"So we wait."

"I guess we wait."

"You can't call him?"

"I don't know his number. Hell, I don't even know if Sullivan's his real name."

"It probably isn't, at that. Look, Brady. Himself won't be altogether thrilled with that quarter-million sitting around losing interest. I'll fill him in as soon as he wakes up. We'll decide what to do next. Why don't you call back around eight-thirty or nine? Either you can talk to him, or I will have discussed it with him. Okay?"

"Sure." I hesitated. Ollie *had* dismissed Perry before dragging me into his vault to see the Dutch Blue Error. "I didn't know you were this interested in the Dutch Blue Error, Perry."

"It's family business. I have to be."

"Um-hm," I murmured.

"If Sullivan calls in the meantime, let me know."

"I will. But don't expect it. He's been a stickler for punctuality so far. Well, we'll see."

Perry and I exchanged good-byes. I tried to turn my attention to the will on my desk. My concentration was poor. I smoked several Winstons, had another cup of coffee, and studied the Boston skyline through my office window.

Around five-thirty Zerk wandered back into my office. "Need me for anything?" he asked.

"Moral support." I waved my hand at

him. "Begone. It's already been a long day. I can't understand it."

"Sullivan not calling?"

"Yeah."

At that moment, the light on my telephone console began to flash. Zerk and I exchanged glances. I picked up the receiver, at the same time punching the button that would permit Zerk to hear both ends of the conversation."

"This is Albert Dopplinger," said the voice. "What's going on, anyway?" A muted hum of conversation, an occasional clink of china, and a Mantovani of violins filtered in behind Dopplinger's voice. "I'm here. I got the message to call you."

"I tried to reach you at the museum," I said. "You'd left already, I guess. Our friend never called, so I was unable to complete the arrangements."

"They're terrible about telephone messages. I keep asking for a phone in my lab. Some problem with cables, they keep telling me. They've offered me half an office. On the second floor. Can you believe that? A five-minute walk from my lab. But I do need a phone. Ah, well ... Will you still want me?"

"Oh, sure. When the times comes. How can I contact you?"

"My home phone. Number's in the book. Very few Albert Dopplingers in Cambridge."

"Okay, then."

"Well. Guess while I'm here I'll have another Bloody Mary. The sea's calm today. Wish Mr. Weston was picking up the tab, though."

"That," I told him, "can be arranged, I'm sure."

I hung up and looked at Zerk. He stood and walked toward the door. "You coming?"

"Think I'll wait around for a little," I said.

"Still think he's going to call?"

I shrugged.

"He won't, you know," said Zerk as he closed the door behind him.

And he didn't.

Ollie wasn't particularly upset when I talked to him Tuesday evening. He seemed preoccupied, as if he had more important things on his mind than a mere quarter-million-dollar business deal.

But when we talked again Wednesday morning, with still no word from Daniel F. X. Sullivan, Ollie seemed quite particularly upset.

"Goddamit, Brady Coyne!" was how he put it. "You find that son of a bitch and you stuff that money down his goddam Irish throat. I want that stamp!"

"How'm I supposed to do that, Ollie?" I said. "I don't know his number or his address or any known acquaintances. I don't know what he does for work or where he hangs out or where he went to school. I don't even know his name, for God's sake."

"How do you *know* you don't know his name?" said Ollie quietly.

I stopped. "Hm. Good point. I'll get back to you."

To Zerk I said, "Want to play private eye?"

He squinted suspiciously at me. "Say what?"

"Private detective. See if we can find our Daniel F. X. Sullivan in the phone book."

"Sweet Jesus," he muttered. He fixed me with a lopsided grin. "They'll be calling me Sam Spade, eh?"

I rolled my eyes. "Thank you," I said.

An hour later I walked out into the reception area. Zerk had his jacket thrown over the back of his chair. His tie was pulled loose and his collar hung open. He was speaking into the telephone. "I'm terribly sorry, Mrs. Sullivan. I had no idea . . . Yes, of course, I'll tell him if I see him, but . . ."

He shrugged and hung up the phone. I

cleared my throat. Zerk turned to glower at me. I sensed briefly what opposing quarterbacks might have felt when they stood over their center calling signals and happened to glance across the line at the Tufts middle linebacker, number 48 on your program, Xerxes Garrett.

Zerk did not look happy.

"*That* Daniel F. X. Sullivan ran off with a nursery school teacher two months ago. Last heard from in Des Moines, where he used his credit card. Five kids at home, oldest nine, youngest three months."

"Can't say I blame the guy," I said.

Zerk ignored me. "Two Daniel F. X. Sullivans are dead. One for several years, one was buried a week ago Saturday. Another one's a bartender who works night who I woke up. He wasn't pleased. One sells maritime insurance. I spoke with his recorded voice on the answering machine. Not our man. You want me to keep going?"

"How many you got left?"

"In the Boston book? Couple of dozen, I'd say. I haven't even dared to look at the suburban books. You really think we got the right name here?"

"No," I said. "I don't. But we've got to be sure, don't you think?"

"I think this private investigating is

boring. I think I'll be a lawyer when I grow up instead." He smiled at me. "I think I need some help."

"You're right," I sighed. "I'll start in the West Suburban book."

I hung the GONE FISHIN' sign on the door and set to work. I flipped open one thick green directory to "Sullivan." There were six full columns of Sullivans. Somewhere around 600 listings. I counted twenty-seven Daniel Sullivans, three Sullivan, D.'s, and four D. F. Sullivans. There were no Daniel F. X. Sullivans.

I threw the book onto the floor, got up, and walked back to Zerk. By now his necktie was on the floor and his loafers under his chair.

"Hey, Sam Spade," I said. "Forget it."

His ear was snuggled to the phone. He covered the mouthpiece with his hand. "Watch what you callin' me, boy," he growled. His eyes darted to the telephone. "Sh," he said to me.

"There's too many," I persisted. "Forget it."

He waved his hand at me. "Yes, Mr. Sullivan?" he said into the phone. "This *is* Daniel F. X. Sullivan of Seventeen Walnut Drive, Roxbury?" He paused. "No, Mr. Sullivan, this is *not* WHDH and I'm *not* asking you for the cash call jackpot number. The reason I'm calling is . . . Ah, shit. Well, that wasn't him, either. That guy was nine hundred years old, at least. So. You're ready to quit already? You hardly got started."

"I didn't get started at all," I said. "It's too much. There's too many of them."

"You got a better idea?"

"Yeah. Forget it. We've got other clients to worry about."

He shrugged. "Suits me. Can I pretend to be a secretary for a while, now?"

The following morning when I got to the office, Zerk was at his desk looking at Sunday's box scores in the *Globe*. He grunted at me and I grunted at him. I went over and set the coffee to brewing. It was my turn.

"Anything on the machine this morning?" I said.

"It's only eight-thirty. I don't start working until nine. Hurry up with that coffee, will you?"

"You could've put it on yourself when you got in."

"Your turn."

"You can wait, then."

"See where Rice went three for four yesterday," said Zerk.

"They lose again?"

"Stanley blew a two-run lead. It's September. They're dead."

I went into my office, lit a Winston, and moved manila folders around on my desk. I sat down, got up, looked out the window at the morning smog, and went out to check the coffee. It was still burbling. I went back to my desk.

A moment later Zerk barged in, holding the *Globe* in both of his hands and shaking it at me.

"Take a look at this," he said.

He spread the obituary page out on top of my desk. I looked.

"You're too young to be checking the obits," I said. "I want my coffee."

"Here," he said. His finger pointed at a picture of a man's face. Under the picture was the caption, "Francis Xavier Shaughnessey, 1968 photo."

"So? Friend of yours?"

"Take a close look."

I did. Then I bent and looked again.

"I'll be damned," I breathed. "Daniel F. X. Sullivan. That what you think?"

"Gotta be. He was younger in this picture. But you can't mistake that nose."

I shifted my attention to the brief obituary. The headline read, "Francis Xavier

86

Shaughnessey, 66. Former auditor for Commonwealth." I read on:

Francis Xavier Shaughnessey, an official in the State Auditor's Office before his retirement in 1978, died suddenly in his home in Boston last Monday evening. He was 66.

Mr. Shaughnessey, a native Bostonian, attended Dorchester High School and graduated from North-eastern University. He served during World War II in the European Theater of Operations, where he earned two Purple Hearts. He received a field promotion to the rank of Captain during Operation Overlord.

After the War Mr. Shaughnessey was the European field representative for the Gulf Oil Company. Poor health forced him to return to Boston, where he began work in the Auditor's Office. He retired in 1978.

Mr. Shaughnessey leaves his daughter, Deborah Ann Martinelli, and a sister, Elizabeth Shaughnessey Monroe.

A funeral Mass will be said Wednesday at 10:00 a.m. at the Church of the Sacred Heart, Dorcester.

I glanced at Shaughnessey's listing under the Death Notices, and saw that visiting hours would be held from two to four and seven to nine on Monday and Tuesday at the Michael P. O'Reilly Funeral Home in Dorchester.

Zerk had been reading over my shoulder. I looked up at him. "Guess I'll be going to a wake this evening," I said.

"You notice something here?" said Zerk, pointing to the newspaper.

"What's that?"

"It says he died last Monday. That explains why he wasn't at our little rendezvous."

"He was otherwise occupied, it seems," I said. I thought for a moment. "Wonder why they waited a whole week before putting in the death notice. And why wait nine days before having the funeral?"

"White folks sho' does funny things sometimes."

"Somehow I don't think that adequately explains it," I said.

Chapter 5

I found the Michael P. O'Reilly Funeral Home halfway down a pleasant, tree-lined residential street somewhere in Dorchester. It was a big Victorian house needing some paint. But the lawn grew lush and green, and the big maple out front glowed brilliant orange in its autumn plumage, and from the outside it seemed a pleasant enough place for gazing at dead bodies, pondering mortality, and murmuring sympathetic inanities to the bereaved.

I parked out back. There were a dozen or so other cars in the lot, a couple wearing official state license plates. I stepped out of my BMW and walked around to the front door.

A dark-suited young man stood by the guest book in the foyer. He held my eye for a moment, then dipped his head in solemn greeting.

"Good evening, sir," he said. "Won't you sign the book?"

I felt his eyes on me as I bent to scribble my name. I glanced at the signatures of those who had preceded me, but recognized none of the names. When I looked up, I realized the man had been watching me by the way his eyes slid away from my face.

"Thank you, sir," he said, with another bow. "It's the room to your left."

I paused in the doorway to get my bearings. The casket sat on a little platform at the far end of the room surrounded by big sprays of gladioli and carnations. A bald-headed man and a fat woman were kneeling beside it, their heads inclined toward the body inside. Along the left wall, a row of straight-backed wooden chairs sat in a line, most of them empty. The rest of the room was occupied by metal folding chairs arranged to facilitate meditating upon the corpse. Most of them remained unoccupied, as well. The mourners evidently preferred to stand together in small clusters, conversing in hushed tones – to facilitate their escape, it seemed to me.

I was anxious to verify whether this Shaughnessey was, in fact, my friend Daniel Sullivan. I moved along the row of chairs against the wall, stooping to take the hand of an elderly woman who clutched a lace handkerchief in her lap.

"I'm so sorry," I muttered, or something

similarly lame. I was grateful that the woman neither looked up nor bothered to respond.

Then I found myself standing by the coffin looking into the paraffin face of Francis X. Shaughnessey. The phrase, "They did a real nice job on him. He looks so natural," came to my mind. They had done a good enough job so I could tell that this Shaughnessey had undeniably been the Daniel F. X. Sullivan of my acquaintance. Beyond that, he resembled all the other examples of the mortician's art I had seen. He was a piece of wax sculpture somewhat smaller than life. It always startled me how bodies laid out in caskets could remain so motionless.

And, of course, he didn't look "natural" at all. He didn't look as if he had ever lived. His mouth had never smiled or sneered, his nostrils had never twitched, his eyebrows had never lifted or frowned. There had never been wrinkles playing at the corners of his eyes and mouth. Blood had never rushed to flush those rouged cheeks. Even his nose seemed to have been reshaped into someone's concept of an ideal form, although in Shaughnessey's case the ideal had been compromised considerably.

I had the sense that the real Daniel Sullivan was hiding under a mask, smirking at me. As I stared down at his shell, it seemed to me that old Dan Sullivan had somehow had the last laugh on me. Not only had he conned me into participating in this barbaric ritual of "visiting" his eviscerated husk, but he had also managed to win our little cat-and-mouse game with the Dutch Blue Error. No matter the price of his victory.

I imagined the eyes of the others in the room upon me, so I knelt beside the body and rested my forearms on the railing. "Where's that stamp, you old rascal?" I whispered.

After I had knelt there long enough to have recited a couple of Hail Marys and a leisurely Our Father, I stood and moved away from the coffin. I figured if I slid inconspicuously toward the back of the room, I could ease myself out without anyone's noticing. My mission had been accomplished.

Then I felt a hand on my arm. "I'm Deborah Martinelli. He was my father."

Vanilla skin, shiny black hair worn long and straight, high cheekbones, and gray eyes like polished silver. With makeup she would be beautiful, I thought. She wore a black sheath which hinted at roundnesses that were not revealed. Her grip on my arm was firm.

"Brady Coyne," I said.

She steered me toward the back of the room, away from her father's body. We sat on a couple of folding chairs.

"I don't know you." Those pewter eyes searched mine.

"No. We'd only met recently. We were in the middle of a business transaction."

She nodded. "You and a hundred others. He was always in the middle of a business transaction. Do you sell paintings?"

I smiled. "No. I'm an attorney."

"Ah," she said, as if that explained it. Her eyes drifted away from my face. I figured she had done her duty, greeting me, and it was time for me to leave. Which suited me fine. I had found out what I needed to know.

I started to stand. "Well, Mrs. Martinelli..."

"Stay a minute." It was a command. I sat down again.

"I didn't know him that well," I said, "but..."

Her head jerked up. Her eyes were razors. "Then don't say something insincere, Mr. Coyne."

I shrugged. "I just..."

"You were going to tell me how natural he looks, maybe?"

I gave an embarrassed little laugh.

"Matter of fact..." I waved my hand. "No. Of course not."

She glanced over at her father's body for a moment, then swiveled her head around to look at me. "Barbaric, isn't it?"

"Well, it depends." I sounded like a lawyer, even to myself. I could equivocate with the best of them.

"We're supposed to be Catholic. This is how we're supposed to do it. We genuflect, we mumble our little prayers, the priests come in, the men go out back and drink, the ladies cry, and somehow it's supposed to make a difference." She shook her head. "But it doesn't. Dead is dead."

"I don't handle death very well, myself."

"I don't *want* to handle death well," she said. "Especially my father's."

"You seem to be doing okay."

"Do I?" Her smile was ironic. "Good. I'm glad I seem to be. Because I'm not. If I was doing well I'd feel sadness, wouldn't I? Or emptiness. Loss. I should cry. But you know what?" She squinted her eyes at me. "All I feel is mad. I am really pissed off that my father is dead. Is that doing fine?"

I shrugged. "Maybe it is."

She tossed her head. "Yeah. Maybe."

I hesitated. "Look. I'm not very good at this. To tell the truth. I just came here to see

94

if your father was who I thought he was, that's all, and . . ."

"And was he?"

"Yes. And beyond that, I don't know what to say to you. Just, I'm sorry."

"Well, at least you're not telling me how God works His will in wondrous and mysterious ways, and that my father now lies in peace with the angels – and all the shit I've been hearing lately."

She smiled quickly when she said the word "shit," as if she thought it might shock me. It didn't.

"That doesn't help much, does it?" I said.

"Makes it worse. He's dead, and now he looks like papier-mâché, and that's that." She cocked her head. "What did you mean about seeing if he was who you thought he was?"

I sighed. "The truth is, your father owns – owned . . . he had a very valuable item which I was helping a client of mine to purchase from him. It was a very complicated transaction, and for reasons of his own, your father chose not to tell us his real name. I know this isn't the best time, but . . ." I reached into my jacket and took out one of my business cards. "This is my card. I'd appreciate it if . . ." I let it hang there.

95

She took my card and seemed to stare right through it. Her fingers moved over the embossed letters as if she were reading braille. Then she looked up at me.

"You came here to do business," she said, her voice flat.

"Well, no, but . . ."

"Maybe we should work out a deal right here, huh?"

"I hardly think . . ."

"*I* think," she said, standing up suddenly, "that you should get the hell out of here right now, Mr. Lawyer."

I stood. "I'm sorry."

"God damn it, just get out of here!"

I shrugged, and as I turned to go I felt a strong hand on my shoulder. "C'mon, pal," said a deep voice. "Come with me. Let's leave the lady alone."

I turned to look into the smooth face of a man several inches shorter than I. He had chocolate eyes, thick, curly hair, and a bushy black mustache. His shiny white teeth seemed to be smiling at me.

"Get that shyster out of here, Philip," said Deborah Martinelli. "This son of a bitch is trying to do business here, and the body isn't even cold."

"This way, buddy," said the man named Philip, and I allowed myself to be let out of the room and across the hall into a smaller room where several men were standing around smoking and talking quietly.

He released his grip on my arm and held out his hand to me. "Phil Martinelli," he said. "Son-in-law of the deceased. Estranged husband to that hellcat. Don't mind her. She's basically hysterical in the best of circumstances."

"I didn't mean to upset her." I fished out a Winston and lit it. I noticed that my hands shook a little.

"Want a little nip?" said Martinelli.

"Well, sure, I guess so."

I followed him to a low table in the corner where four other men had gathered. "Excuse me," he said to them. "This man needs a drink."

He poured an inch of Cutty Sark into a clear plastic glass and handed it to me, and I didn't have the heart to tell him I'd have preferred bourbon. I took it in one gulp, trying to focus on the fire in my stomach while ignoring the taste in my mouth. Martinelli took the glass from me and refilled it.

"Didn't catch your name," he said.

"Coyne. Brady Coyne."

"Friend of Frannie's then."

"Sort of."

He touched one of the other men on the arm and said, "Doc, I'd like you to meet one of Frannie's friends." To me he said, "This is Doc Adams."

He was a graying, vigorous looking guy with washed-out blue eyes and a crinkling smile. I took his hand.

"This is Mr. Coyne," said Philip. "Deborah just evicted him from the wake."

"Brady Coyne," I said. "Nice to meet you, Doctor."

"Doc is okay. Or Charlie. Mary – that's my wife – calls me Charlie. But, Jesus, not Doctor. Please."

"Doc, then. You were his . . .?"

"Hell, no. I just messed around in his mouth a little. Full set, uppers and lowers. He liked the way I made him look. Wanted me to tinker with his nose when I was done with his teeth. I declined. Beyond redemption, his nose. Fran mainly liked the medication I prescribed for the pain."

Doc Adams waited, an expectant grin playing at the corners of his mouth. Martinelli chuckled. "Two shorts of Cutty, straight up, every four hours, as needed. Right, Doc?"

"Absolutely. The secret to my surgical success. I am very popular with my patients."

"Understandable," I observed.

"I'd be happy to introduce you to these other chaps," he said, "but I'm afraid we haven't exchanged names."

One of them turned and said, "We don't really know each other, either. Just met. Our mutual friend is in the other room." He held out his hand to me. "I'm Schwartz. This is, ah, Remington – right? – yeah, and Bertinelli."

"Bertelli," corrected the eldest of the three.

"Whatever."

"Coyne," I said, shaking hands with each of them. They were all older than me. Schwartz I estimated to be in his mid-fifties. He had a thin, fox face and a dark beard streaked with gray. Remington I guessed at sixty – an ex-athlete gone to fat, with a thick neck and bulging shoulders. Bertelli was short and dark and wrinkled and bald. I recognized him as the one I'd first seen kneeling beside Shaughnessey's casket.

The little room was windowless and oppressive. Doc Adams dropped his empty plastic cup into a waste basket, nodded and waved to us, murmured a few words to Martinelli, and left. I wanted to follow him, but instead I followed the example of the

99

others and opened my shirt collar and jerked loose the knot of my tie.

"Damn tragedy about Frannie," said Remington to no one in particular. "Damn tragedy." Remington, I guessed, had knocked back several shots of Scotch already. The flush on his face was from more than the heat of the room.

"You never know," said Bertelli. "I read where this math professor at B.U. got killed in his own home – fancy place in Winchester, I think it was. Turns out the guy was a faggot and he'd go down to the Combat Zone picking up sailors, whatever, and bring 'em home, and sometimes they'd stay with him for a few days. He'd give 'em clothes, buy them presents. All the time nobody had any idea. Except his wife. She knew all about it. So this one time he makes the mistake of bringing the wrong guy home."

"Frannie wasn't like that," said Martinelli.

"I didn't mean it that way," said Bertelli. "Just that you never can tell what's gonna happen to a guy. That's all I meant. I didn't mean nothing about Frannie. You know, they said that math professor got stabbed something like forty times. Blood all over the place. Wife found him. They never did find the guy who did it. I'm not saying nothing about Frannie. It's just, you know, you think you know a guy . . ."

I didn't know what they were talking about, and it must have showed in my face. "You knew what happened to Frannie, didn't you?" said Martinelli to me.

I shrugged. "I just saw the obit in the paper."

"Well, Deborah didn't want it mentioned in the obituary. Frannie was murdered. The story was in the papers when it happened."

"I missed the story," I said. Actually, I vaguely remembered seeing something. But because Shaughnessey's name didn't mean anything to me at the time, I hadn't made the connection.

"Yeah," said Martinelli. "Poor Frannie. Back of his head all bashed in. Police are saying they think it was some kid looking for drugs or money. Or maybe both. Black guy was seen in the area. His apartment was turned upside down. Stuff from the medicine chest all over the place. Course, they don't know what was taken. Guy busted a window on the first floor. They figure Frannie came home and surprised him." Martinelli turned to Bertelli. "Frannie wasn't like that professor. He didn't have weird friends."

"That explains it," I said.

"Explains what?"

"Why his daughter ..."

"Why Deborah is out of sorts?" Martinelli laughed. "She's not out of sorts. Believe me, I know. That's the way she is. A bitch. Don't feel bad."

"Still, it was stupid of me to mention anything to her."

"Mention what?"

I hesitated. "Oh, just a small business transaction. Nothing, really. Certainly nothing that should be discussed at a wake. If I'd had any idea he had been murdered ..."

"Hey, forget it," said Martinelli. "Like I said, that's just the way she is."

"What sort of business are you in?" said Schwartz to me.

"I'm an attorney."

"Frannie in some sort of trouble?"

"He wasn't my client." I lit another cigarette.

"Hey, I didn't mean to pry." Schwartz put his hand on my arm. "I had business with him, too."

I shrugged and sipped the Cutty Sark. It tasted awful, mainly because it didn't taste like bourbon. I put down the plastic glass and turned to leave. I'd heard enough, and the stifling heat of the little room was beginning to make me nauseous.

The young man in the dark suit still stood by the book in the lobby. I nodded to him on my way out.

"Mr. Coyne," he said,

I turned around. "Yes?"

"You don't remember me, do you?"

"I'm sorry, no."

"It was three, four years ago. I was a patrolman then. I testified for the husband in a custody case. You represented the mother."

I shrugged.

"You remember. The woman had stabbed the guy in an argument. They were divorced, and he was trying to get custody of the kid. I was the one who arrested her. What I remember about the case was that I told this story about how she was so violent and had attacked the guy with a paring knife – I mean, what kind of a mother could she be, stabbing people with knives? – and you didn't even cross-examine me. Man, there was blood all over that kitchen. She slashed his arm a couple of times. Nothing really serious. But all that blood. How'd that case turn out, anyway?"

"We won."

"No kidding?"

"Sure." I smiled. "Your testimony was a big help."

He frowned. "But I was testifying for the other side. For the husband who wanted the kid back. Your client was the mother with the knife."

"And a very good mother, too. As your testimony helped us establish. Protecting her baby, her nest, at all costs. Risking her life for her child. She'd have fought to the death for that child, just as you said. A fanatically devoted mother. I remember you, now. You did a good job."

He grinned. "I wondered why you didn't cross-examine."

I smiled. "No need. You'd said it all. So you're a detective now, I gather."

"Right. Investigating this Shaughnessey case."

"Checking out the folks who come to the wake, eh? You figure the person who killed Shaughnessey will come here?"

He shook his head. "No, not really. This is pretty much a guaranteed waste of time. The captain's bright idea. We've got this pegged as your average B and E. Some kid broke in and lost his head when Shaughnessey got home. Smashed him too hard. Place was in a shambles. We haven't got much to go on. Assume there's some drugs missing. He had prescriptions for Valium, and we couldn't find any Valium in his place, so we assume that was taken. Probably money, though we don't know, of course. Otherwise, we know of no motive. One of those random things. Daughter's been no help whatsoever. A black guy was seen outside the building that evening, not that that means a hell of a lot."

"But you'll check out everyone who comes to the wake?"

"Yes. And the funeral."

"You'll make sure everybody can account for his whereabouts the night of the murder."

"Yes."

"And you'll ask about their relationship with the deceased."

"Right."

"And you'll end up eliminating everybody as a possible suspect."

"Doubtless."

"And then you'll write it off and get back to work on your other cases."

"I didn't say that, Mr. Coyne. We're looking for a black male, mid-twenties, six feet tall . . ."

"Come off it," I said.

He smiled. "We'll do all we can. Really."

"I suppose so," I said. "I didn't catch your name."

"Leo Kirk. *Lieutenant* Leo Kirk."

"When you get around to checking me out," I said, "I do have something you might find relevant to this case." I gave him my card.

"What kind of something?"

"Shaughnessey owned something valuable, that's all."

"Is it missing?"

"I have no idea."

"You think someone murdered Shaughnessey so that they could steal this what-ever-it-is? What *it* it, anyway?"

"A postage stamp."

"Yeah?" Kirk cocked his head at me, then shrugged. "Okay. I'll get in touch with you."

Chapter 6

I passed up Shaughnessey's funeral on Wednesday. I knew I'd have to talk to his daughter sometime. But I didn't really look forward to it. And I felt pretty certain that she wouldn't greet me with hugs and kisses at her father's funeral.

On Thursday I thought of calling her. Then I decided I'd give her a few days to recover from her ordeal. So I shuffled manila folders around on my desk for a while and selected a separation agreement that I should have finished a week ago. My client, the wife, wanted use of the summer place in Osterville for the season. Her husband wanted to split it, a month each. My client contended that the family had always gone there together, that the children should be at the Cape for the summer as they always had been, that the custody agreement did not provide for the husband to have the kids for a whole month at a time, that they certainly couldn't live together for a month, and that therefore he could visit them at the Cape for his weekends but that she, the wife, should be allowed to live there for the entire ten weeks.

I thought I had a pretty good case. Her husband's attorney thought he was in good shape, too. We'd iron it out over martinis and a big chef's salad at Locke Ober's. There was no hurry. Summer was ten months away. I inserted a couple of commas and changed a few "whereas's" in the document and took it out to Zerk for typing.

He was on the phone. When he saw me he gestured with his free hand to the telephone. "It's for you," he mouthed.

"Who is it?"

Zerk covered the phone with his hand.

"A lady. Wouldn't give her name. I asked real nice, too. I asked was it business or personal, and she told me it was none of *my* business, just let me talk to Mr. Coyne, if you please. Sounds personal."

"Sounds unpleasant," I said, and I went back to my office to take the call.

"This is Deborah Martinelli. Francis Shaughnessey's daughter. And no, I'm not calling to apologize, nor do I expect you to have the grace to apologize, either. My father was buried yesterday and I now have his affairs to disentangle and I came across your card in my purse. If you had business with my father, what was it?"

She sounded breathless, like an inexperienced actress reciting her lines too rapidly. She also sounded angry. I didn't like it.

"You *are* a tough cookie, aren't you?" I said mildly.

"I beg your pardon?"

"For all you know," I said, "I could be a very nice person. For all you know, I could be your father's long-lost brother. Hell, for all you know, I might have an opportunity for you to make a quarter of a million dollars without lifting a finger."

"Somehow I doubt any of that, Mr. Coyne. Can you just tell me what it is you want?"

"The only definitely untrue thing is, I'm not your uncle. Thank God. Some people actually think I'm a reasonably tolerable person. Not my ex-wife, although that in itself might be considered an endorsement. And as for the quarter-million, that's what I wanted to talk to you about. Of course, if you'd rather rant and rave . . ."

She hesitated. "Okay. Talk." Her voice sounded a shade less hostile. Just a shade.

So I talked. I told her about the Dutch Blue Error, carefully avoiding the use of Ollie Weston's name. I told her that her father had used a fake name, that he had been

109

scrupulously careful about his dealings with me, and that I remained prepared to pay a quarter-million dollars for the stamp.

"And you think whoever killed him was after the stamp," she said.

"I don't know. Seems possible. I'd like to find out."

"I knew about the stamp," she said. "He picked it up overseas last winter. He was very pleased with himself. He kept it locked away. Out of harm's way, he liked to say. Ironic, huh? He said it would bring him lots of money. He was always doing that – buying and selling things."

"Locked away," I repeated. "Where?"

"Why should I tell you?"

"You don't have to tell me. I don't care where it's hidden. I'd just like to buy it from you. Why don't you go and get the stamp, and we'll arrange for my client to buy it."

She was silent for a long time. I could hear her breathing. I lit a Winston and waited.

"I haven't been back there since he died." The hostility had drained out of her voice completely, replaced by a flatness that suggested an effort at control.

"Where?"

"His place. His townhouse. I'm not exactly thrilled at the idea of going there."

"Well, I can understand that."

"Oh, can you really?"

"Matter of fact, yes," I said. "I think I can."

"Somehow," she said, "I doubt if you can, Mr. Coyne. Not unless you happen to have stumbled upon your father's body lying in the middle of his living room with the back of his head all smashed in and blood all over the place, and his arm twisted around funny so that you can see right away that he's dead, and when you bend over to look at him his eyes are staring right at you." She paused. "You ever do that?"

"No. I never did. I'm sorry."

"Well, I did. So I'm not looking forward to going back."

"Maybe if you brought your husband."

"Philip? No, not Philip. We're not together. Philip and I are negotiating a divorce, as you lawyers like to say. That, by the way, did not please my father. He adored old Philip. Wanted to talk me out of it. That's why I went there that night. So he could talk me out of divorcing Philip. Which he would not have succeeded in doing. So, no. I'm not asking Philip."

"A friend, then."

"I don't have that kind of a friend."

I resisted the temptation to tell her that I didn't find that surprising. "How about a policeman? The detective who was at the funeral, maybe. Kirk. I'm sure they've been through the place already."

"Oh, I imagine they have," she said, sounding tired now. "No doubt they've been through it all. Messing up the underwear in his bureau, rolling up the rugs, digging through his papers. No. I don't want a policeman with me."

"Well..."

We were silent for several moments. When she spoke, the businesslike energy, the hostile edge, had returned to her voice. "What are your rates, Mr. Coyne?"

"You can't afford me."

"Oh, I expect I can."

"I gear my rates to the desirability of the case, Mrs. Martinelli. You can't afford me."

Surprisingly, I heard her laugh. "You know, you're a real prick."

"That," I said, "may be the nicest thing you have ever said to me."

"Not for hire, huh?"

"Nope."

"Damn."

I hesitated. Unbidden, the image of those unworldly, silver eyes flashed in my mind. "I might do you a favor, though," I said.

"You might?"

"Yup. And you wouldn't even have to ask nicely, either."

"You'll go with me?"

"Sure."

"Just to be friendly?"

"Yup."

"Hey, okay. That's nice. Thanks."

"Don't go getting all syrupy on me, now. I wouldn't know how to deal with that."

"I'll try to be careful. So, then. What time is good for you?"

"Tomorrow morning? Around ten?" I glanced at my desk calendar to verify. "Yes, that would be a good time for me. Shall we meet there?"

"Fine. Ten is fine." She gave me a Mt. Vernon Street address. Beacon Hill. Very swank, old Boston. I didn't realize they let Dorchester Irish onto Beacon Hill. Times change. I jotted the address onto a scrap of paper, asked her for her own address and phone number, and learned that she lived way out in Carlisle, a little rural community west of the bedroom suburbs of Boston. Also a nice address, Carlisle. People in Carlisle owned horses, sent their kids to the Fenn School, thence to Wellesley and Amherst, played polo, and traveled to Europe a lot in the winter to ski.

"The stamp is in the house, then," I said.

"In a strongbox, yes. If it's still there."

"Well, we'll see."

"Tomorrow at ten. Yes."

"Okay. See you then."

Friday morning carried the promise of one of those perfect New England fall days – crisp and clear, with the faint hint of an east wind wafting in off the ocean to blow away the city smells. It was a great day for golf.

I checked into the office and told Zerk he was the boss for a while. Then I headed for Beacon Hill on foot. I strolled down Newbury Street past the tony shoe stores and little restaurants. I crossed over to Beacon Street at Dartmouth, and then down Charles Street at the foot of the Hill. I paused to look into the windows of the antique and craft shops and successfully resisted the impulse to go into a little place that sold old books.

I turned right and began to climb Mt. Vernon Street, marveling as I always did at the evidence of the high-density canine population on the Hill. I watched a couple of cops clap a Denver boot on a green Mercedes and then grin and shrug their shoulders at a guy in a neatly trimmed white beard and three-piece suit who hustled out of one of the narrow brick buildings to argue with them.

I found the address Deborah Martinelli had given me. It was quarter of ten. I sat on the front steps to wait for her, figuring that if she was anything like her old man, she'd arrive on the dot of ten. But before I finished a cigarette, a red Karmann Ghia pulled up and she stepped out.

At first I didn't recognize her. In my mind's eye I still saw an angry woman in a black shift, her face pale and her mouth a bitter slit. This Deborah wore jeans and running shoes and a bright yellow sweatshirt. Her dark hair fell in soft waves, framing a perfect oval face. She wore pale pink lip gloss and a touch of eye shadow.

And that mouth even attempted a smile when she saw me waiting for her, although her eyes did not participate. It was the cautious smile of someone who understands that the reasons for smiling are transitory at best, while the sadnesses keep coming back.

"I'm sorry," she said, a little breathlessly. "Am I late? I hope you haven't been waiting long. The damn traffic on Storrow Drive – and there's construction around Fresh Pond, you know ..."

"Just got here," I said, standing up.

She held out her hand. "Thank you for coming." The smile faded. She climbed the steps ahead of me and fumbled with some

115

keys. "I haven't been back here since that night," she said. "I haven't exactly been looking forward to it." The door pushed open. "Well, come on in."

We stepped into a tiled foyer, beyond which I saw a large, airy kitchen. Copper cookware and rush baskets and potted ferns festooned the big beams that intersected on the ceiling. Butcher-block counters, dark-stained cabinets, three shelves of cookbooks, tall stools, and every electrical gadget and machine imaginable. On one wall was a huge open fireplace. At the rear of the room, morning sunlight streamed through double French doors, in front of which stood a round oak table. It was right out of *Better Homes and Gardens*, and I told Deborah Martinelli so.

"He had the whole house done over when he bought it. Gutted the whole thing down to the beams and brick walls. He loved it here. There are four floors, one room to a floor. This one, the kitchen. Next one up is the living room. Then the library, as he called it. And the top floor was his bedroom."

"Where . . . ?"

"Where did I find him?" She exhaled a long breath. "In the library. On the floor." She touched my arm. "Come on. We

116

came for that stamp. We've got to go upstairs."

The stairway was one of those steep, iron-corkscrew affairs. I followed her up, more aware than I wanted to be of her jeans stretching across her rump and the way her sweatshirt rode up over her belt to reveal a peek at the flesh of her narrow waist.

The living room on the second floor had been decorated in muted shades of white and beige, which set off the several brightly colored paintings and lithographs that hung on the walls. The room was dominated by an enormous fireplace against one wall and an abstract painting bigger than a king-sized bed hanging opposite it. The furniture had been arranged so that it focused on a soldered iron sculpture of a woman engaged in some sort of physical contortion. It looked like a bowling trophy that had gone through a garbage disposal and then been buried in the ground for a few years.

"His *objets d'art,*" she remarked with a wave of her hand as she led me to the next staircase, this one a wide, wooden affair. "He had no particular love for them. Called them a hedge against inflation. Do you like them?"

"I'm a Norman Rockwell fan, myself."

"Umm," she said, meaning, I gathered, "That figures."

I followed her up the stairs. When she got to the top, I heard her gasp and I held out my hands in a reflex as she lurched back against me. "Jesus," she whispered.

I moved beside her. My hand remained on her waist. She stood rigidly and stared into the room. It lay in shambles. Books had been swept from their shelves, furniture was overturned, lamps knocked over, and broken glass lay scattered on the carpet. But that wasn't what caused her reaction. On the yellow rug near the fireplace I saw a large, brown stain, and I knew instantly what it was.

It was Francis Shaughnessey's blood.

"I thought someone would've cleaned it up. Dumb, huh?"

She stepped away from me. "What a goddam mess," she said.

"Is this the way you found it?"

"Yes. I think so. I didn't study it." She turned to face me, a little smile betraying her emotions. "You don't analyze things too carefully, you know, when you find your father lying dead on the floor. You scream maybe once, and then you remember nobody's going to hear you, so you kneel down beside the body and you realize that it's hopeless and that he's really dead, so you call the police and go downstairs and make

118

a cup of tea and wait for them. And then you answer a lot of questions and let them take you to the station so they can ask you a lot more questions. And then you tell them you're okay, you're fine, and they drive you back to your car and you drive home. And then you wait for yourself to start crying."

"Look." I reached to touch her.

"Forget it. I'll go get the stamp."

She disappeared up the last flight of stairs to the bedroom on the fourth floor. I wandered around Francis Shaughnessey's library. I visualized the police experts going through it, vacuuming here and there for bits of lint or dirt or hair, dusting for fingerprints, taking photographs, formulating hypotheses. And concluding that it had been the work of a drug-crazed burglar.

They hadn't known about the Dutch Blue Error.

She was gone for a long time. When she finally returned, she said, "Let's go downstairs to the kitchen. I'll make us some tea."

I followed her back down the two flights of stairs and sat at the kitchen table by the French doors, through which I looked out over a tiny garden surrounded by high brick walls grown over with vines. A little fieldstone path wound among some perennial plantings and shrubs. There was one metal chair and a chaise longue and a gas grill. I had my balcony overlooking the harbor. Shaughnessey had his own little island of solitude.

Beside the latch on one of the doors I noticed that a pane of glass was missing. Tiny shards still stuck out of the frame. This was how the murderer had broken in, I guessed.

Deborah brought me a big mug of tea. "Microwave ovens are marvelous," she said. "Boil water in an instant."

It wasn't tea at all, but some exotic herbal concoction. No caffeine. Still, it was delicious.

She sat across from me. "It wasn't there," she said, her gray eyes staring at me.

"The stamp?"

"Yes. He kept it in his strongbox. Hidden in the bedroom. The strongbox was still locked, everything else was there, all in order. But the stamp is gone."

"He must've kept it somewhere else."

"No. He kept it in the strongbox."

"A safe deposit box, maybe. Maybe after he saw us that time with the stamp he didn't put it back."

She shook her head. "No. I told you. He'd have put it back in his strongbox."

"Then it was stolen."

"The strongbox wasn't touched." She brushed her hair away from her face with a quick, nervous motion of her hand.

"Are you sure?"

"Yes. For Christ's sake, don't interrogate me."

I lit a Winston and pondered this information. Francis Shaughnessey had been murdered in his home. He owned a stamp worth a quarter of a million dollars. He kept it in his home. It was missing. It hardly seemed likely that those facts were unrelated.

"Don't smoke in here," she said.

"You kidding?"

"I hardly ever did. Take it outside, if you have to smoke."

I shrugged. She wasn't kidding. I stood and unlatched the glass-paned door.

"This," I said, pointing to the missing panel of glass, "must be where the alleged perpetrator made his entry."

"You're talking like a policeman," she said. "Which is almost as bad as talking like a lawyer. I've had enough of both." Her eyes softened. "Yes. That's what they seem to think. That's how he got in."

"He would've had to climb the walls around the garden, then."

She shrugged. "Take the cigarette outside, will you?"

I went out and sat on the chaise. It was a pleasant, quiet spot. The morning sun streamed in over the high, ivy-covered walls. Several of the shrubs had been pruned and trained in the Japanese bonsai manner, each a miniature work of art set in a garden of white pebbles and artfully located rocks. Clusters of deep red and rust-colored mums provided strategic spots of color. Fragrant thyme grew among the stones of the walk.

Beyond the garden walls on all sides rose four- and five-story buildings. Each of them, I imagined, opened onto a similar little island.

After a few minutes, Deborah came out and sat in the chair. She handed me my mug of tea. "You forgot this. I warmed it up for you."

"Thanks," I said. "You trying to be nice to me?"

"My mind must have been wandering. It won't happen again."

"See that it doesn't," I said.

She shrugged. "So what now?"

"I don't know. Be nice if we could come up with the stamp."

She nodded. "It would. Somehow I'm going to have to pay Philip off."

"He wants alimony?"

"Not alimony. Philip and I pooled our

savings to start up my business. Ten thousand dollars four years ago, plus some bank loans. It was a one-person real estate office in Concord then. Well, me and a part-time secretary. Philip never had a thing to do with it except for that initial investment. Now I've got seven other women working for me – four brokers, one salesperson waiting to take her broker's exam, a full-time secretary, and an accountant. We own the office building we're in. And I'm negotiating to set up a branch in Littleton and another in Acton." She looked sharply at me. "I *want* to buy out Philip, it's not that. But he won't accept his original share. He wants what he thinks is his share of the worth of the business. Half. Take the past couple of years, our projections, our investments – we're computerized for MLS, very up-to-date – he figures that comes to a bit over two hundred thousand. Not bad for a five-K investment four years ago, eh?"

"Not bad indeed."

"So his lawyer is putting on the pressure. My business is not very liquid. My capital is tied up. You can't grow with a lot of liquid lying around. I have a big debt to manage, and don't want to take on another big one to buy out Philip."

"Well, now you have your father's estate."

She looked sharply at me. "What's *that* supposed to mean?"

I spread out my hands. "Only that now you should be able to take care of Philip."

"Exactly what are you implying?" Her silver eyes snapped.

"I'm not implying anything," I said. "Just pointing out the obvious. Hell, this house alone..."

"This house, Mr. Coyne, is heavily mortgaged. My father ran up big bills with the decorators. Beacon Hill townhouses don't move easily these days. The city's reevaluating. Taxes are skyrocketing. Don't you try to tell me I'm better off now that my father is dead."

The idea was startling to me, and her eyes, while they were staring intently into mine, seemed to twinkle in ironic amusement, as if the joke were on me. I made a show of looking for a discreet place to flick the long ash that had gathered at the end of my cigarette. I found a patch of bare dirt behind a white rock. When I looked back at Deborah she was smiling.

"Well, anyway," I said casually, "I hope you're getting good legal advice."

"My, you *are* an ambulance chaser, now, aren't you?"

"Like I told you, you can't afford me. I don't want your business."

She waved her hand. "A joke. I don't even trust lawyers."

"Me neither," I said. "But I would like to buy that stamp for my client."

"If I can find it, you can buy it," she said.

I took my cigarette butt back into the kitchen, stuck it under the faucet to make sure it was out, and tossed it into the fireplace. Deborah latched the French doors behind her.

"Aren't you afraid someone else will break in?" I said.

She flapped her hands. "My father said this was perfectly safe. No one could get in, he said. The walls outside are too high. And the back is completely surrounded by buildings. It's a whole maze of walled gardens out there. Someone would have to come from someone else's garden, over the walls, to get in through here."

"Someone did," I observed.

She nodded. "So it seems." She smiled ironically. "He loved these French doors."

She stood there, staring out the doors, lifting the hair off the nape of her neck with both hands. Without looking at me she said, "He thought he was so safe. And then someone smashes in his skull."

"What," I said softly, "did he get hit with, do you know?"

She turned to face me. Her smile was both wistful and ironic. " 'The Dreamer.' A piece of sculpture. It happened to be the one thing my father kept because he liked it. It was created for him by an artist he knew. It was pieces of scrap iron welded together. That's why he kept it in his library. The things he cared about he kept there. The police have it now."

" 'The Dreamer,' " I repeated.

"It was an abstract, of course."

"Yes, of course," I said.

She shivered. "Can we go now?"

We walked out of the building. She locked the front door and offered me a ride in her Karmann Ghia. I declined. She climbed in and rolled down the window. "I do appreciate your coming," she said, peering up at me.

"My pleasure," I said.

"Sure," she replied, nodding. "The pleasure of my company, and all that."

I grinned, and didn't answer.

"For someone who's basically a bastard, you're a relatively easy bastard to get on with," she said.

"You're too kind."

I was standing beside the car, my hand

resting on the ledge of the opened window. Deborah put her hand on top of mine. "You know, I feel a little better. It's funny, but knowing that there's a reason for this, that it wasn't some random thing, a freak – it helps. Does that make any sense?"

"Yes, I suppose it does. We're assuming it was the stamp."

"That is what I assume," she said firmly.

I moved my hand away from hers. "Why don't you hire someone to go in there and clean up?"

She bent forward, fumbling with the ignition key. Then she started up the engine. She looked up at me. "I will. And I'll call you if I find the stamp."

"Do that," I said. I turned and started walking back to my office.

I read recently that the island of Manhattan has twenty thousand restaurants. I figured out that a person who started at the age of twenty taking his dinner in a different restaurant every night of the week would be seventy-five by the time he went through all of them. By which time, of course, there would be several thousand new ones to try.

I don't have the figures to prove it, but I'd guess that a man would have the same problem sampling just the Italian restaurants

127

in and around Boston. I tried it a few years ago and gave up. There are too many, and too many of them are good.

I settled on Marie's, a little cellar five steps below street level just outside Kenmore Square. It's the only place I need to know to appease my periodic cravings for pasta. Marie scribbles her daily offerings on a blackboard. She has twelve little tables with red and white checked tablecloths lined up along the brick wall. The smells when you walk in are enough to reduce Mahatma Gandhi himself to a slobbering glutton. You can't get pizza there, or fancy veal entrees. Mainly pasta and sauces and breads and pastries and good beer and wine. Marie hires B. U. undergraduates to wait on tables. Her sons do most of the cooking nowadays, but Marie is always there to supervise and greet her "guests," as she calls us.

Leo Kirk and I met at Marie's in the afternoon after I'd seen Deborah Martinelli. He had already eaten. I had a spinach linguini al dente with a light clam and squid sauce, and a bottle of Heineken's. Kirk settled for a cannoli and a cup of espresso.

He seemed singularly unimpressed with my revelation that Shaughnessey owned a priceless postage stamp. Nor did the fact that it appeared to be missing cause him to lift his eyebrows. "Not the sort of thing one keeps around the house," he said.

"The daughter said he kept it there."

Kirk shrugged. "We've got this one pretty well buttoned up."

"You've got a suspect?"

He smiled at me. "No, we haven't got a suspect. We've eliminated several. It boils down to what it always looked like."

"Routine B and E, huh?" I said. "Shaughnessey's upstairs, the guy whacks him on the head, then tosses the place for pills and money."

"Yeah. Like that. Or maybe Shaughnessey comes home when the guy's there. Either way."

Our waitress was leaning across the table next to us lining up the salt and pepper and cheese shakers. Kirk eyed her skirt as it rode up the back of her thighs.

"Assume the guy was looking for the stamp," I said.

Kirk sipped his espresso and continued to study the waitress's legs.

"Either he found it, or he didn't," I persisted. "Doesn't matter. Maybe he beat the shit out of Shaughnessey to get him to tell where it was."

"No sign of that," said Kirk quickly. "Just the blows to the head."

"Blows?"

"Why, yes."

"More than one?"

"According to the M.E. there were three. Any one of them would've killed him. Hit with a statue. One of those abstract things that looks like an outboard motor mounted onto a Frisbee. Heavy. Big cast-iron base. Three whacks to the back of the head. And, yes, it was wiped clean of fingerprints."

" 'The Dreamer,' " I said. "That was the name of the statue. Anyway, I don't see how you can eliminate the stamp as a motive so easily."

Kirk sighed. His dark eyes stared up at me over the rim of his cup. "One of the things we learn in police work is that ninety-nine times out of a hundred things turn out to be exactly what they seem to be. What looks like suicide usually *is* suicide. A guy who looks guilty to us usually is – even when some smart lawyer gets him off. This looks like a robbery that went bad. Guy panicked. Stamp or no stamp."

"Some kid looking for drugs," I said. I remembered Deborah Martinelli's words. "A random act. A freak."

"Right. Drugs or money. Hell, there were valuable works of art in that place. None of them were gone. Most places that are broken into, there are valuable things around. So Shaughnessey had a stamp, and you can't find it. Not too hard to hide a little stamp, eh? Anyway, you said yourself that no one even knew he had it."

I sopped up the sauce on my plate with a hunk of bread, wiped my mouth, and lit a cigarette. "You finished with the daughter now?"

"Yes. Unless something else turns up."

"Which is unlikely, right? I mean, this case is headed for the inactive file. Eventually you'll nab some kid and he'll confess, you hope. Or maybe you'll get lucky, and someone's snitch will put you onto somebody. In the meantime, you're all overworked and underpaid and have higher-visibility crimes to solve."

"Look, Mr. Coyne. This stamp thing is pretty farfetched. Hey, if it turns up, then it'll look different, you know? But let's face it. We haven't got anything to go on. What do you expect me to do?"

"I don't know," I said. "That's not my job."

"We find a guy, it's your job to get him off, am I right?" Kirk smiled darkly. "Whether it's some crazy lady slashing her old man with a paring knife or a hopped-up delinquent looting somebody's home for money and drugs."

I nodded. "My job right now is simple. I want to buy a stamp for my client."

"Funny way to practice law."

"I agree," I said.

By the time I got back to the office Zerk was gone. He left me a note propped up on his typewriter. "Call Massa Weston. I got a dinner date tonight. Went home to wash my armpits. See you Monday."

I mourned, briefly, the bleak weekend I faced. I'd lug home a stack of those manila folders, dump them on the table by the sliding glass doors that looked out over the harbor, and feel their accusing eyes on me every time I walked past them. I'd spend Saturday morning in the laundromat. Peanut butter sandwich for lunch. Try to make a dent on the stack of folders in the afternoon. Maybe take a nap. Saturday night I'd eat alone, then argue baseball with my friend, Pat, the bartender at the Shamrock. We'd evaluate the hookers who plied their trade there, and Pat would try to persuade me to verify our assessments. I'd decline. Sunday afternoon I'd catch the Patriots on the tube. Then back to the manila folders.

I had no reason to wash my armpits.

I went into my office and phoned Ollie Weston. I had been putting it off. Ollie did not receive bad news with equanimity.

He expelled a loud breath into the telephone when I told him that Francis X. Shaughnessey, a.k.a. Daniel F. X. Sullivan, had been murdered in his Beacon Hill townhouse, and that the Dutch Blue Error he owned was missing.

"God damn it, Brady."

"It's gone, Ollie. What can I tell you?"

"So find it, for Christ's sake."

"That's, ah, not my line."

He sighed. "I know. Listen. You figure the murderer got the stamp?"

"I'm leaning that way. The police aren't."

"Okay." He paused for a moment. "Okay," he repeated. "We're in good shape, actually. Whoever got the stamp must be smart enough to understand the same thing that Sullivan, or whatever his name was, did. That it's no good unless he sells it to me."

"I don't know, Ollie."

"Of course you do. It's simple. Sooner or later he'll come to me with the stamp. That's why he took it."

"Maybe. *If* someone took it."

"If no one took it, then eventually what's-her-name will find it. Same difference."

"I'm glad you're taking it so well, Ollie."

133

"What've I got to lose? If the stamp never turns up, I'm where I was before I knew there was a second Blue Error. Owning the most valuable postage stamp in the world. And saving two hundred and fifty grand, by the way. If it does turn up, it'll be mine anyway. Either way, we're golden."

"Unless the guy who took it goes public with it."

"He won't. Anyone smart enough to go after the stamp is smart enough to bring it to me. Anyway, going public means a murder rap."

"But not if he goes to you."

"We can work that out," said Oliver Hazard Perry Weston. "Don't worry your head about the Dutch Blue Error, Brady."

"Ollie, as your attorney, I have to warn you . . ."

"No you don't," said Ollie sharply. "I said not to worry."

"Okay," I said. "I won't."

Chapter 7

Several work days passed. I thought about the Dutch Blue Error very little. Ollie Weston said I didn't have to, and I always try to do as my clients ask.

Zerk went to Washington, stayed three days, and returned grouchy. He also did a hell of a job for me on a patent search. When I told him so he growled at me.

I was at my desk, finally making an impression on that stack of manila folders, when Zerk stuck his head into my office. His forehead was wrinkled and his mouth turned down in a quizzical grimace.

"Phone for you," he said.

"Who is it?" He usually buzzed me from his own desk.

"Dopplinger."

"What's he want?"

Zerk shrugged, and closed the door. I picked up the phone. "This is Brady Coyne," I said.

"Can you come over here?" Dopplinger's voice was low, as if he were afraid of being overheard.

135

"Why? Where are you?"

"At the museum. I'll be in my lab. I can't talk to you now. Please hurry. Come now."

"Can't you tell me what this is about?"

"Just hurry. Please." I heard the click of the receiver.

"Be back," I said to Zerk on the way out. He looked up from his papers, stared at me for a moment, and nodded.

I decided to drive over the river to the Peabody Museum. I figured the traffic wouldn't be too bad in the early afternoon. I was wrong, of course. The Metropolitan District Commission, in its infinite wisdom, had selected that very day to repaint the lines on the road that passed over the B. U. Bridge. To make matters worse, an MDC cop was directing traffic.

I found a parking place on the street only a block from the Peabody Museum. I took the front steps two at a time, recalling the urgency in Albert Dopplinger's voice. It had been more than an hour from the time of his call to the time of my arrival.

I took two wrong turns in the bowels of the museum before I found myself in the corridor two floors below ground level. As they had been the other item I was there, all the doors were closed. This time I noticed that each door had a name stenciled in tiny letters above the knob. I found the one that said DOPPLINGER, A. and knocked softly.

When there was no answer, I knocked again more loudly and called, "Albert. It's me. Brady Coyne. Open up."

I tried the knob. The door was unlocked. I opened it slowly and called, "Albert. Are you in there?"

The big room was dark. I could make out the black, eerie shapes of scientific apparatus silhouetted by the light that filtered in from the open doorway. I stepped into the room and felt along the wall for the light switches. The fluorescent lights fluttered, then blinked on brightly. Shadows were suddenly transformed into objects – microscopes, lamps, test-tube holders, glass vials and containers.

And Albert Dopplinger.

He lay behind the long island that bisected the room. I saw his feet first. I moved quickly to him. He was on his stomach, his legs splayed apart. One side of his face rested on an arm, which was curled under him. His eyes were closed. The other arm reached straight out. I bent over him.

"Hey, Albert. You okay?" I touched his arm, then shook it. He didn't respond. I picked up his glasses, which lay by his elbow. One of the lenses had been broken. I knelt beside him and placed two fingers under his jaw. I felt no pulse. I pressed harder, and still could find nothing.

Then I saw the hole in his head – a neat, round, empty little hole just above the hairline at the base of his skull, a tiny black eye staring blankly at me. I touched it gingerly, and my finger came away red.

I sat back on my heels, squeezing my hands together between my thighs and hugging my elbows against my ribs to control the quivering that began to travel up my spine to the back of my own neck.

"Jesus...," I whispered, and barely finished pronouncing the curse – or prayer – when my jaw was snapped backward and the breath was cut from my throat and a suffocating blackness covered my face. "Sorry, pal," said a voice. I tried to claw my way free to breathe, and the pressure on my throat increased. I was aware of loud breathing, and grunting sounds, and I couldn't tell which were mine. Sweet-tasting fumes invaded my mouth and nose and burned into my lungs, and suddenly the pain disappeared and red and yellow lights flashed and faded and I felt myself sinking gratefully into a deep, painless sleep.

It was a sleep full of images and sensations. I seemed to float, then sink. I rode waves, climbing up toward consciousness where the images became clearer, then falling back into a soft, gray fog. There were voices and distorted faces – faces with eyes that seemed to melt and drip down cheeks like broken eggs. I tried to hold myself at the crest of a wave, and a voice said, "Take it easy. Relax. Let it go." And I did let it go, and plummeted back into the bottomless black pit.

After a while the images and the voices and the motion went away, and I slept.

When I awoke and opened my eyes, the light stabbed my pupils like sharp needles, and I squeezed my eyes quickly shut. I moved my head and heard myself cry out in surprise. "Oh!" And then it became a groan, as the blade of pain became a generalized hammering ache in my neck and the back of my head.

I tried opening my eyes again. Cautiously, I lifted my eyelids a millimeter, and then another. The blurred face of my dear, dear friend Xerxes Garrett hovered over me. I closed one eye, and his face, wrinkled with concern, came into focus.

"Oh, shit," I moaned.

"Take it easy, man. You're okay." Zerk's

139

hands were on my shoulders, moving me into a sitting position. I realized we were in my car. Zerk sat behind the wheel, and I was sprawled on the seat beside him. "You think you can sit up so I can move out of here before a cop comes along?"

I started to nod. I stopped myself quickly when someone pounded a spike into my head. "Sure," I whispered.

"Let's go."

He started the car, and we began to move. That was when my stomach began to pound into my diaphragm like a big, powerful fist, and I vomited magnificently into my lap.

"Oh, Christ, man," said Zerk.

"I'm sorry," I moaned.

"We gotta keep going now," he said. "Think you can open your window?"

I managed to roll down the window. I lay my head back against the car seat, my eyes closed. Cambridge air had never tasted as sweet as that which blew in through the window of my BMW as Zerk maneuvered down Mass Ave and out Boylston to Memorial Drive.

"I'm gonna take you home, my man," said Zerk. I sighed in reply, and with my head back and my mouth open and my lap full of my own puke, I slept.

I remember Zerk dragging me from the

car in the garage in the basement of my apartment building. I remember him wrestling me into the elevator, and the young woman who squeezed in with us before the door slid closed, and Zerk saying to her, "My friend here had a bit too much to drink, you know."

She got out on the very next floor.

Zerk hauled me into my shower and held me under the armpits while cold water poured over both of us. We stood there, fully dressed, the freezing water slowly driving the fog from my brain. I tried rolling my head around on my neck and found only an aching stiffness there. I looked at Zerk, his dark face grim, his brown eyes staring intently into mine, the water sitting in big droplets in his short, thickly curled hair and dripping from his nose and chin.

"That's a good suit you've got on, there," I said to him.

"I'll send you the cleaning bill," he replied. "You might consider burning yours."

"You gonna tell me what happened to me?"

"Later. Right now, why don't you get your clothes off and get yourself a proper shower. I'll make us some soup."

"No soup."

"Not hungry?"

"Oh, I'm hungry," I said, feeling better by the minute. "Matter of fact, now that you mention it, I'm famished. But I don't have any soup."

"What kind of a place do you live in, you got no soup?"

"I've got lots of frozen dinners. Or beef stew. I think there's a can of Dinty Moore's in there."

"God!" muttered Zerk. But he left me to my shower. I adjusted it to a comfortable warmth, stripped off my clothes, and lathered myself up, as if I might wash away all the pain and sickness and dirt. Before I stepped out I actually found myself humming. It was an old Turtles tune. "Happy Together." Boy, it felt good to feel good!

I was buffing my back with my big, soft towel when I noticed my face in the mirror, and my face reminded me of the other face I had seen, the one with the long banana nose and the closed eyes, and that reminded me of the little black hole at the back of Albert Dopplinger's skull, and that was when I felt the bile rise again in my throat.

I knelt by the toilet and gagged and hacked and finished what I had started in the car. I flushed the toilet and rested my head on the seat for a minute. Then I stood and rinsed out my mouth and splashed cold water onto my face.

Zerk tapped on the door. "You nearly done?"

"I think so."

He opened the door and shoved my old wool bathrobe at me. "Put this on and come out, then. Beef stew's hot."

"I, ah, think I'll just have some tea. If you don't mind. Please."

I heard Zerk chuckle and close the door.

Zerk was wearing one of my flannel shirts and a pair of old Levi's he found on the floor of my closet. The shirt stretched tight across his chest, and the cuffs came halfway up his forearms. The pants fit him fine, except they were perhaps an inch too short. He sat across from me at the trestle table in my combination living-dining room. I looked out past him toward the Boston Harbor. I figured a large part of my monthly rent (recently jacked up by several hundred dollars) paid for that view. It was worth it. I never tired of it. The sun had set behind us. The water lay still and black as carbon paper, but the sky still glimmered with the after-light of daytime. Specks of green and yellow and red lights blinked on the surface of the harbor. Running lights. Boats making port. Here and there the flash of white sails appeared, skidding and darting like water bugs.

Zerk gobbled all the beef stew. I sipped my tea cautiously. It seemed to settle all right. I stirred in a teaspoon of honey and drank more boldly.

"You gonna tell me all about this, or what?" I said.

"You have to thank me for saving your life, first."

"Thank you. So what happened?"

He wiped his mouth with a paper napkin and downed a big swig of Schlitz from a can he'd found in the refrigerator. "After you left this afternoon, I sat there for a while, like a dutiful secretary. But I couldn't get the tone of Dopplinger's voice out of my head. Did you notice it?"

"Yeah," I said. "Scared. Or nervous, at least. Urgent."

"Right. Real urgent. Anyhow, I probably sat there half an hour, and then I said the hell with it, I'm going over there. So I hopped the subway. Took forever, naturally. When I got to the museum I went right to Albert's lab. Figured that's where you were headed. The door was closed. I knocked, and when no one answered I tried the knob. It was unlocked, so I went in. I flicked on the lights.

You and Albert were lying there, side by side, and I thought you both were dead."

"We weren't, though."

"*You* weren't. He was."

"Right. I remember."

"Very dead. Shot neatly in the back of the head. Once. No exit wound. A thirty-two, I'd guess. Judging from the burn marks, the gun was pressed right against his skull. It'd make almost no noise that way."

"An execution," I said.

"Like that, yeah," said Zerk. "So, anyhow, I lugged you the hell out of there. Luckily, I'd noticed where you left the car on my way to the place, so I fished the keys from your pocket and managed to shove you in. People hardly looked at us. Guess lots of folk go to the Peabody Museum in the afternoon to get loaded. I waited around for a while till you decided to wake up and blow lunch. Then I brought you home. And here we are." He appraised me, his eyes crinkling into the beginning of a grin. "You didn't see the guy, huh?"

"No. He said something to me – 'Sorry, pal,' I think it was. Something like that. The voice sounded vaguely familiar. Then ..."

I got up and took my mug of tea to the sliders and gazed out over the dark ocean. An airliner passed in front of me in its landing pattern, heading over to Logan. A couple of big ships showed their lights. It calmed me. It always did. I slid the doors open to let in some fresh air. It smelled of fog and seaweed. It was warm for September. Rain was in the air. I stepped out onto my little wrought-iron balcony. Zerk followed. We each sat on a plastic and aluminum folding chair. I put my feet up on the railing, and I felt the damp breeze blow up under my bathrobe. It felt good, that cool breath of the sea.

"I'm going to have to make sense out of all this some time," I said. "I mean, he was in some kind of trouble. Albert."

"Um-hm."

"And he called me." I paused. Zerk said nothing. "Query: Why did he call me? Why *me?*"

"You asking me for an answer?"

"Hell, yes, I'm asking you for an answer."

"Okay," said Zerk. "Then, hypothesis: You're the first lawyer he could think of. He had a legal problem. Accused of a crime, threatened with a lawsuit, whatever. Wanted advice, wanted counsel."

"Hm," I said doubtfully. "Could be."

"You think it had something to do with the stamp, don't you?"

"I don't know. Yeah, it's a good hypothesis."

146

"It is," nodded Zerk. "Then the question becomes: *What* did it have to do with the stamp?"

"The stamp's missing. Albert found it."

"Therefore?"

I shrugged. "Therefore, he called me. To tell me. Shit, Zerk, I don't know."

"Keep a couple things in mind," he said.

"Like what?"

"Like, when he called you, he was scared. That, in retrospect, seems very reasonable because, in the second place, somebody assassinated him."

"If Albert had the stamp . . ."

"Yes."

"Somebody murdered him for it," I finished. "Possibly the same guy who killed Shaughnessey."

"Very possibly."

"And now that person has the stamp."

"In which case," said Zerk, "we should be hearing from him."

"Which explains why he didn't kill me."

"I was wondering about that one," said Zerk.

"Okay," I said. "This is good. Let's keep going. There are other possibilities. Begin with different premises. Like, *if* it had to do with the stamp, but if Albert *didn't* have it. Where does that lead us?"

147

Zerk was silent for so long I didn't think he had heard me. By now it was completely dark outside, except for the faint glow of city lights that lent texture to the blackness. Finally he said, "If Albert didn't have the stamp, but someone thought he did, they might, you know, torture him, threaten him .."

"Sure. And then, when they're done, kill him."

"Which leaves unanswered the question of why *you* weren't tortured, maybe. And then killed," he added with what I thought was unnecessary candor.

"They didn't have time. They heard you coming," I said.

"In which case you'll be hearing from them. Or him, or whoever."

"Either way. Oh, Jesus," I said, the image of the little black hole in the back of Albert's head flashing in my brain again.

"There's another possibility," said Zerk slowly. "Suppose all of this had something *else* to do with the stamp – something based on a premise other than the one which holds that Albert had the stamp, or knew of its whereabouts."

"Like what?"

"I don't know. Maybe the guy who killed Albert already had the stamp, and wanted

148

Albert to authenticate it, and then had to shoot him to protect his secret."

"That doesn't make much sense," I said. "Whoever had the stamp has stolen property, and, most likely, a murder on his hands already. He'd lay low for a while. Besides, the authentication of a dead man isn't much good, I wouldn't think. It could never be used."

I heard Zerk yawn. "Yeah, maybe. This is better than patent law. But it's tiring. Think there's another Schlitz in the fridge?"

"Help yourself," I said. "I'll have one, if there's two in there."

He returned in a moment and handed me a can. I placed it against my forehead. The shock of its icy touch made me sit up a little straighter. Zerk took his seat again and lifted his feet up onto the railing beside mine.

"One thing's for sure," I said, after we had sat in silence for a while, sipping our beers.

"What's that?" said Zerk lazily.

"We've got to go to the police."

"Why?"

"Because, my friend, we are lawyers, and a crime has been committed, and it's our obligation to justice to go to the police. That's why. And you know it."

"But . . ."

"Never mind. This is fundamental. We

149

may be considered suspects, ever think of that? Hell, I left the scene of a crime. So did you. And you are the one who removed me from that scene. The cops right now are probably looking for a big black guy who dragged a half-conscious white guy out of the museum at or about the estimated time of the crime. Our fingerprints are probably all over the place. The door knob. The light switch." I tilted my head back and took a long swig of Schlitz. "So if you don't like the lawyers doing their duty to the cause of justice argument, try some of those others. Self-preservation."

"Sure. Okay. But..."

"But, nothing, damn it. We go. First thing in the morning. We should go tonight, actually. But I feel shitty. We go together and we tell them everything."

"Even about the stamp?"

"Everything. Of course. We tell the truth. We leave out nothing. Understood?"

"Sure," he said softly. "Understood."

We finished our beers in the damp, dark silence, high above the Boston Harbor. The night air caressed my thighs under my bathrobe. I thought of Deborah Martinelli. Then I thought of her father. Then Albert. Victims. Two men had been murdered now.

I wondered if there was any way any of it could possibly be unrelated to the Dutch Blue Error.

Chapter 8

"I been up all night with this fuckin' thing. Why the hell they can't find bodies at the beginning of my shift, I don't know. It's always at the end. Or else in the middle of the goddam night, and they gotta call me at home. You sure you don't want some of this coffee? I mean, it's terrible – pure mud, you can feel it rot your stomach. I don't blame you." Lt. Cornelius Mullins, Homicide Inspector for the Cambridge police, ran his fingers through his thinning black hair. His necktie was askew, and his collar hung open. His shirtsleeves were rolled halfway up his thick forearms.

He rubbed the palm of his hand across his mouth, as if he were trying to wipe off the black stubble of his beard. Then he pinched the bridge of his nose, squeezing his eyes shut. "Okay. So what do you know about this thing, anyway, Mr. Coyne?"

I summarized for him the events of the previous day – Albert Dopplinger's telephone call, my arrival at the museum, Albert's dead body, the attack on my person, and my rescue at the hands of Zerk. Mullins kept his eyes closed while I related my tale. He slouched in his chair, his head back. He looked as if he were sleeping.

"How long did you say it took you to get there?" he asked, his eyes still shut.

"To the museum? An hour, at least. There was a big traffic jam on the B.U. Bridge."

"So you arrived at what time?"

"I told you. Around three, I'd guess. I didn't check."

"And what time did the deceased call you?"

I flapped my hands. "Little before two, I'd say. Zerk could probably tell you."

Mullins opened his eyes. "I imagine they're asking him," he said.

They had separated me and Zerk as soon as we told them why we were there. Inspector Mullins had led me down a long corridor lined with doors with opaque glass windows. Two uniformed policemen had taken Zerk in another direction.

"Why did he call you?"

"Albert? I don't know. He didn't say. Just, like I told you, that it was urgent."

"Was that his word?"

"He said he wanted me to hurry. His tone was urgent."

"So what do you think was urgent, that

he should call you? You said you hardly knew him."

"I don't know."

"Did he say he wanted a lawyer?"

"No. Not like that."

"And you'd only met him once."

"Right. And we talked on the phone once, too."

"So why did he call *you?*"

I shook my head. "I told you, I have no idea."

"What about this stamp you mentioned? Did it have something to do with the stamp?"

"Look, Inspector," I said. "I'm a lawyer, and I know you have to do what you're doing. But I told you everything. I didn't need to come here. But I did. Voluntarily. I don't appreciate being treated like a suspect. If I can help you in any way, I'd be happy to. But don't interrogate me." I paused. He was leaning forward, looking at me, his elbows on his desk and his chin resting on his fists. "I'm not a suspect, am I?"

He snorted through his nose. "Of course you are. You know that. Everybody is. Don't worry about it. What I'm trying to do is, I'm trying to see if there's something you forgot to mention, see, something you didn't tell me

154

that's clanking around up there in your head somewhere, in your subconscious, that maybe I can help you to remember if I ask the right questions. And, sure, if you start contradicting yourself, then I'll start wondering about you. So. What about this stamp, now?"

"I don't know if this had anything to do with the stamp or not, except that was the only context I knew Dopplinger in. As I told you, the man who owned the stamp was murdered, and no one seems to know where it is. I don't see how Albert Dopplinger fits into that. Except he knew about the stamp, and he was murdered, too. I surely don't see how *I* fit into that, except that I'd like to buy the stamp for my client."

Mullins rested his forehead in a bowl he made with his two hands. It didn't look like he'd be able to finish our interview. Without looking up at me, he said, "Why did your friend go to the museum?"

"Zerk? I don't know. I guess he felt uneasy."

"Uneasy?"

"Yes. He answered the phone when Dopplinger called."

"Does Mr. Garrett always follow you when you visit distraught clients?"

"Dopplinger wasn't my client."

155

"Has Garrett *ever* followed you like that before?"

"I never had a phone call like that before."

Mullins's head snapped up. *"Has* he?"

I frowned at him. "No. He's never followed me like that before. But . . ."

"How long would you figure it'd take him to get to the museum by subway?"

"Oh, half an hour, maybe. Depends."

"And by taxi?"

"If he went by the B. U. Bridge, over an hour, yesterday. Usually fifteen, twenty minutes. Look, Inspector, what're you suggesting here?"

"Nothing," said Mullins. "What do you think I'm suggesting?"

"All these implications about Zerk. He was worried about me. He came and rescued me after whoever was in that laboratory gassed me. He came here voluntarily, just like I did. He's an attorney. You're trying to make him into a suspect."

Mullins smiled tiredly. "I told you, Mr. Coyne. Everybody's a suspect. Okay. I'll level with you. We have a witness who said he saw a black man who fits Mr. Garrett's description lurking around the downstairs area in the museum about the time the murder would have occurred. *Before* three. Before you got there. I'm betting our witness

156

can identify your friend. You already told me that Garrett knew where Dopplinger's lab was located. He could have buzzed over there way ahead of you. Hell, Mr. Coyne, it could've been Garrett who chloroformed you, for all you know. He might've been in that room all the time."

"Zerk? Come on. That's ridiculous."

Mullins shrugged.

"Is he being held?"

"He came here like you did. To help the police investigate an apparent homicide. That's all."

"Because if he is, he's got the right to have an attorney present. I want to be present."

"He's just telling his story, Mr. Coyne. Just like you. He'll be informed of his rights if it's necessary." Mullins heaved himself to his feet and lumbered to the coffee pot which sat on a hot plate in the corner of his office. "Sure you don't want some of this? Naw. You don't. Vile stuff. Can you think of anything else?"

I thought for a moment. "What about Albert's notebook? Anything in it?"

"Notebook?"

"He carried a notebook in his pants pocket."

Mullins shrugged. "We didn't find any notebook."

157

I sighed. "Probably in his office or something."

Mullins leaned forward and peered at me. "You feeling okay today?"

"A little shaky," I admitted. "What'd you say you thought it was? Chloroform?"

"I imagine so. They – he, whoever shot Dopplinger – chloroformed him first. Damned if I know why. We found a saturated rag in the room. Place was full of chemicals, of course. You know anybody who owns a twenty-two caliber weapon, Mr. Coyne?"

Mullins knocked me off balance with his abrupt change of subject. I couldn't tell if he was being careless and unstructured, or if he was a clever interrogator. I was beginning to suspect the latter.

"No," I answered. "No – wait a minute. Look, I don't know many people who own guns, period. I have one, but I keep it in my safe in my office. It's a thirty-eight," I added quickly. "But this man who died – Sullivan – Shaughnessey, that is – he had a twenty-two. Or at least he *said* he had one. Is that what killed Dopplinger? A twenty-two?"

"Evidently. So it appears. That's preliminary. They'll dig the slug out of his head and know for sure. Just by looking at the entry wound, they can pretty much tell."

"I would have said it was bigger," I said. "A thirty-two, maybe."

"You examined lots of bullet holes in people's heads, Mr. Coyne?"

I smiled. "No, not many."

"So Shaughnessey had a twenty-two, you say." Mullins seemed to ruminate on this piece of information. He looked as if he was chewing up his tongue. "Well, it's doubtful Shaughnessey killed Dopplinger, now, isn't it?"

I nodded. "Doubtful."

"I'd like to come up with Shaughnessey's gun."

"Maybe I can get it for you," I said.

"Oh?"

"I know his daughter. Shaughnessey's daughter."

"Safe to say, Mr. Coyne, that if she can put her hands on that gun, it won't be the one we're looking for. Still, I'd appreciate it. Mr. Garrett have a gun?"

"No. I don't know. Not that I know of." I tapped out a Winston and lit it. "You're on the wrong track. Zerk didn't do this."

"Oh, I don't think he did. I just don't think he didn't, yet, either."

I nodded. Mullins rolled his shoulders, groaned, and began to rummage among the chaotic mess of papers on his desk.

Somewhere among them he found a half-smoked cigar. He crammed it into his mouth and lit it. The little office was immediately filled with the smell of burning peat. "Nothing like a good cigar," sighed Mullins.

"It's because he's black, isn't it?" I said.

"Who? Mr. Garrett? Why, yes, I guess in this case it is."

"What do you mean, in this case?"

"In *this* case, Mr. Coyne, our witness saw a black man. If your friend Mr. Garrett was white, we probably wouldn't give him a second thought."

"I explained to you why Zerk was seen there."

"Yeah, yeah. I know." Mullins blew a big cloud of smoke at the ceiling. "Look, we appreciate your coming here, Mr. Coyne. Saved us a lot of trouble."

"Trouble?"

"Sure. Trying to identify you and bring you in and all."

"Me?"

"Oh, sure. We got several witnesses saw you. Didn't I mention that?"

"No."

"Oh, well. You'll be around if we need you, huh?"

"You mean, don't leave town."

Mullins waved his hand. "Nah. You

160

know. Something might come up. I might think of something to ask you. That's all."

I took a business card from my wallet and handed it to him. He glanced at it and flipped it onto his desk, where I figured it would be devoured by the chaos of papers there. "You can go, Mr. Coyne," he said. I stood. Mullins remained seated. I leaned across his desk to shake his hand. His grip was limp. He rubbed his eyes with his wrist. "Christ, I gotta get some sleep. Some racket this is. I shoulda been a lawyer." He waved me out with the back of his hand. "Be in touch. Close that door behind you, will you?"

I went back down the long corridor to the open area by the front desk. I couldn't find Zerk. After several minutes of waiting for the desk officer to get off the telephone, I managed to learn that Zerk was still being questioned, and, no, he wasn't being held, why don't you have a seat if you want to wait for him.

The longer I waited, the angrier I became. I imagined they were grilling him. I had about decided to demand that I see him when he appeared. One look at his face told me to move him fast. I grabbed his arm and pulled him outside the station.

"Mothafucks," he muttered. "Oh, those mothafucks!"

"Take it easy," I said. "Let's get some coffee."

He allowed me to steer him to a little coffee shop around the corner from the police station. We sat across from each other in a booth. A sleepy waitress brought coffee without being asked. "Anythin' else, boys?"

"Just the coffee," I said. "Thank you."

"Bastards," spat Zerk. "They want to put me in a lineup."

"They didn't, did they?"

"No. They want me to come back."

"Not without your lawyer, you won't."

"My lawyer?"

"Me."

He stared at me for a moment, then lowered his eyes to his coffee cup. "Yeah," he mumbled. "Honkie law. Maybe I should get myself a black lawyer."

I thrust my face across the table at him. "What the hell is *that* supposed to mean?"

Zerk glared at me. "They puttin' *you* in a lineup? Tell me something. Did they call *you* 'boy' in there? They ask *you* if you had a record? They tell *you* they were going to check you out in Akron? They ask *you* where you were at such and so time, if *you* owned a gun? They question *your* sexual preferences, Counselor?"

I shook my head. "Mostly, no," I said

162

softly. "It was nothing like that, Zerk. Shit, friend, I'm truly sorry."

He nodded. "Yeah. Me, too. I'm truly sorry I ever let you talk me into going there."

"You had to. Somebody saw you there."

"Sure. But somebody saw *you* there, too."

I nodded. "Yes. Somebody did."

"But you're not going into any lineup."

"No. I'm not."

"Mothafucks." Zerk sipped his coffee, his face dark and furrowed. "The law. Justice. Piss on it."

I lit a cigarette and sipped my coffee. Zerk was silent. We avoided each other's eyes.

Finally I said, "Look. I've got to know some things."

His eyes shifted to meet mine. "Things?"

"Yes. Like, what time did you get to the museum? And why did you go there in the first place? And how long were you there before you found me? And where in the museum did you go before you went to Albert's laboratory? Those kinds of things."

"You son of a bitch."

I banged the table with my fist. "God *damn* it, will you listen to me! You were there. And they're looking for a black man who fits your general description for the Shaughnessey murder. Sooner or later the Cambridge cops and the Boston cops are going to put their heads together and make a connection."

"My 'general description.' Yeah. A black man. Period."

"You'll have trouble making a civil rights case out of it, my friend."

Zerk pondered his coffee cup for a moment, then he looked up at me. "Yeah. Okay, so you're right. Now what?"

"For now, I'm your lawyer. I'm rusty as hell on criminal law, Zerk, but if you're really in any trouble, I'll get you the best damn lawyer in town. In the meantime, I can take care of your rights."

"Yeah. Okay."

"It's the least I can do for the man who saved my life."

"I didn't save your fuckin' life," he said. But he looked into my eyes, and the creases in his face seemed to smooth out a little. "Wouldn't save your honkie life, Counselor. Not worth saving. No sir. I just didn't want to lose a good job. That's all. Watching out for old number one."

I smiled. "You're learning. Learning fast."

Two days later Leo Kirk showed up at my office. He was accompanied by a dumpy guy named Stone with big jowls and no hair, whom he introduced as his partner.

164

"Kirk and Stone," I said. "Sounds like a law firm."

"Would that it were," said Kirk gloomily. "I hate having to work for a living."

Stone puffed a little cigar with a plastic grip. It was dwarfed in the vast, red expanse of his face. "Let's not fuck around, Leo," he said. He kept the cigar clenched in his teeth when he talked. "Let's just get to it."

"Let me guess," I said. "You've decided that maybe Francis Shaughnessey wasn't murdered by some random burglar. You've been talking to Mullins in Cambridge. You want to ask me a few questions."

"Not quite," said Kirk. "Actually, we want to ask your associate a few questions. Mr. Garrett."

"You don't need my permission."

"He's right," said Stone. "I told you. Let's just take him along."

Kirk ignored his partner. "This is not, uh, official, Mr. Coyne. We're not accusing Mr. Garrett of anything. We're coming into your place of business, disrupting your routine, and we would like a few minutes of the man's time. That's all."

"Very considerate," I said. "It's all right with me. I can't speak for Mr. Garrett."

"Look," said Kirk earnestly. "As far as I'm concerned, what happened in Cambridge the other day is just a coincidence. I really haven't..."

"*I* don't think it's a coincidence," I said.

"See?" said Stone.

"But Zerk had nothing to do with either of them," I finished.

Kirk sighed. "Well, I don't know. But, see, we got this eyewitness who saw a guy outside Shaughnessey's place that night, and we got a sketch..."

"Black guy," I said.

"Right. Black guy. Big. Six-one, two."

"Curly hair, probably."

"Aw, come on, Mr. Coyne. You know better than that."

"I know that white people see big black guys on the street at night and that's all they see – big black guys. Must be several thousand big black guys in Boston. Many of them can be seen on the streets."

Stone reached into his jacket pocket and withdrew a folded piece of paper. He smoothed it open and laid it on my desk. "Big black guy with a neat little mustache. Looks a lot like Harry Belafonte. Except blacker. And," he added, narrowing his eyes, "our witness happens to be a domestic for some nice rich folks in Louisburg Square. Black lady."

I examined the sketch. It looked like Zerk.

166

It looked a lot like him. The eyes, the hairline, the mouth. I glanced up at the two detectives. "Okay. I'll call him in. If you guys don't mind, I think I'll stay while you talk to him."

Kirk shrugged, and I pressed the button on the intercom.

"Yeah?" came Zerk's voice.

"Come in for a minute, will you?"

"You gentlemen need coffee? Sweet rolls?"

"Cut the shit, Zerk. Come in here, please."

"Yassah," he said.

When he came in I introduced him to Kirk and Stone. He scowled when he shook their hands.

"Couple questions, Mr. Garrett," said Kirk.

"What is this?" said Zerk to me.

"They're investigating the Shaughnessey murder."

"Aha!"

"Where were you on the evening of Monday, September 18?" said Stone.

"I was murdering this guy up on Beacon Hill. I've got this heavy habit, see, man, and I was, see, strung out . . ."

"Don't fuck with us," said Stone, his eyes

squinting through the smoke that curled up from his little cigar.

"Just answer him, Zerk," I said.

"Why?"

I sighed. "We're lawyers. We want to help them solve their case."

"I'm helping. I'm confessing."

"Don't, Zerk."

"They got it all figured out. You know that."

"Do you remember where you were that evening?" said Kirk.

"No."

"Please try."

"Do *you* remember where *you* were that night?"

"We're asking the questions, boy," said Stone.

Zerk turned slowly to face the fat man. "You call me 'boy' again and I'll break open your face. Cop or no cop."

Stone didn't flinch. "I wish you'd try," he said.

"I don't remember," said Zerk to Kirk. "Okay? Want to take me in now?"

"Is there any way you can check? Someone you might have been with – an appointment, a date, someone who might have called you at home?" Kirk smiled apologetically. "Please try to think."

"I don't keep a diary."

"Do you own a gun?" said Stone.

"No."

"Stolen any automobiles lately?" Stone's mouth twitched into a grin.

"Listen, you fucker . . ."

I reached up and held Zerk's arm. "Cool it," I said to him. Then I spoke to Stone. "What are you talking about?"

"Akron, Ohio, March, 1972. One fourteen-year-old juvenile name of Xerxes Garrett was picked up joy-riding in a new Oldsmobile. He didn't own it."

"Aw, man," said Zerk.

"That is not relevant," I said, glaring at Stone. "And you know it."

"You're right," said Kirk. He spread his hands in a gesture of appeasement. "Please understand, Mr. Garrett. You are accused of nothing. Your past is, as Mr. Coyne says, completely irrelevant. We are simply doing our job. We have an eyewitness who provided us with this composite" – he held up the sketch – "and we know you were at the scene of the Dopplinger murder. Not," he added quickly, holding up his hand and smiling, "that you're accused of anything there, either. But, as you can see, looking at this sketch, there is a certain resemblance."

Zerk barely glanced at the sketch. Then

he turned to me. "Do I have to go through this?"

I shook my head. "No. No, you don't." I spoke to Kirk. "I think it's time to terminate this interview."

Kirk nodded. "Yes, I suppose you're right." To Zerk he said, "Mr. Garrett, I'm sorry for this. I hope you understand our position." He held out his hand.

Zerk ignored the proffered handshake. "I understand a lot."

Stone jabbed out his cigar in the ashtray on my desk. "We'll be back, boy. You ain't seen the last of us."

Zerk grinned evilly. "You better have a friend with you when you see me next time."

When the two detectives left, I said to Zerk, "You didn't behave yourself very well, you know."

"I *knew* this was going to happen. I told you when we were in Cambridge that they'd be after me. There's more justice in Little Rock, for Christ's sake, than there is in Boston." He began to pace around my office. "Where were you on the night of so-and-so? Do you own a gun? Stolen any cars lately? What about our eyewitness who actually saw a black man on that very night? Oh, man!"

"What about the car?" I said.

He whirled to face me. "What about it?

170

I'm walking home from the library, for Christ's sake, and my buddy pulls up in a new car and offers me a ride. So I get in and a minute later we're pulled over. What do you call that?"

"Bad luck. Bad judgement."

"Yeah. So I get a juvenile sheet. That's supposed to be buried. So how do these guys find out about that?"

I shrugged. "Simple phone call. Off the record. You know how it works."

"But they can't..."

"In a court of law, if they mention it the case could be thrown out, right. Look. Stone was trying to rile you. You know the drill."

"Damn right I do. What do you think I wanted to be a lawyer for?"

"If you want to be an effective lawyer, you've got to learn to control yourself."

"Easy for you to say," he grumbled. But he seemed to relax. He dropped heavily onto my sofa.

"Look," I said. "Don't worry about it, okay? They're fishing, you know that. About all they've got to go on in either of these cases is what we've told them."

He sighed. "I don't think I exactly allayed their suspicions, did I?"

"No, I guess not."

"So now what do we do?"

"Nothing," I said. "Forget it. Get back to work."

He reached over and picked up the sketch from my desk. "This does look a little like me, doesn't it?" he said.

"It sure as hell does."

Chapter 9

New England Nor'easters come sweeping down the coast driving hard, cold rains ahead of them. When they come in early autumn, the old-timers call them "line storms," since they demarcate the boundary line between summer and fall. Time for the fishermen to haul in their boats, pull in the lobster pots, and hang up their nets for winter mending.

For those of us who don't make a living hard by the sea, line storms remind us to put away our tropical suits, golf-clubs and fly rods.

This one came on the first Sunday afternoon of October. I watched its arrival from my balcony. The clouds began to roll in around noontime, sending the harbor boats scurrying for shelter. By the middle of the afternoon, the clouds were packed in solid, hanging dark and low over the water, which the winds were whipping into a gray froth. The rain came at a sharp angle, low and fast. It moved in from the black horizon, raced across the tops of the whitecaps, and arrived at my apartment building with startling suddenness. It rattled against the windows like a skyful of pebbles.

I poured myself a double shot of Jack Daniel's and sat at my table to watch the storm. Even after it got too dark to see, I remained sitting there, reluctant to get up to turn on a light. I thought of my parents, both dead for many years, and the Sunday evenings of my childhood when we all huddled around the big Philco radio in the living room listening to "The Shadow" and eating popcorn, and I recalled the vague depression that came with the realization that my Sunday evenings wouldn't always be so cosy.

Sometime after eight o'clock I forced myself to get up and turn on some lights. I flicked on the television and dumped a can of Chef Boy-R-Dee cheese ravioli into a saucepan. I put it on a low heat and left it there to simmer while I sipped some more bourbon in front of the tube. What I saw was considerably less entertaining than "The Shadow" – a trick of memory, probably, rather than an objective assessment.

The phone, when it rang, startled me.

"No one home," I said to it.

It kept ringing. I resented its intrusion into my melancholy introspection. I sighed and picked it up.

"This is Brady Coyne," I said in a sing-song voice. "I'm not home right now. If you'll leave your name and number I'll get back to you right away."

"Try to be nice, will you?" It was Deborah Martinelli. "I need to talk with you."

"At the sound of the tone, please leave . . ."

"They broke into my house."

I hesitated. "Are you okay?" I remembered the big brown stain on Francis Shaughnessey's carpet.

"I'm okay. I was out this afternoon. When I got back . . ."

"Was anything taken?"

"No. I don't think so."

"Did you call the police?"

"Well, no. I called you."

"The stamp, do you think?"

"What else? They must've been after the stamp. My place is a mess. They broke the window of my back door."

"Like at your father's place."

"Yes."

"And nothing is missing."

"I said no."

"Call the police, Deborah. That's all you can do."

"And what will they do?"

"They'll come, look around, talk to you. They may try to lift some fingerprints, look for footprints and tire tracks outside. That sort of thing."

"Sure. Right." There was a long pause. "You're not for hire, huh?"

"No."

I heard her sigh. Outside, the rain ticked against the windows. It seemed to come softer, now, no longer driven in brittle sheets by the wind. Way out beyond my window I could detect the line where different shades of gray touched to separate the ocean from the sky.

"Well," she said finally, "I'll call the cops, then."

"That's what you should do."

"Thanks for the advice."

"That's all right."

"Sorry I bothered you."

I didn't answer.

She coughed and cleared her throat. "Look," she said, "I know enough to call the cops. You didn't have to tell me that. I didn't call you so you could tell me that."

I waited.

"I told you why I called. I need to talk with you."

"We can talk."

"God! You don't make things easy." I heard her take a deep breath. "Listen," she said, her voice low and controlled. "The last

176

thing I want is pity. But my father's been murdered. Someone broke into his house and killed him. Today someone broke into my house. I don't feel all that secure, you know? What if I'd been home?"

"They probably timed it so you'd be out."

"Whatever. They found nothing. So they'll be back."

"The police will take care of you."

"You're making me grovel, you know that?"

I hesitated. "Yes. I guess I am."

"You know what I want."

"I guess I do."

I thought of the cold rain and the old warmth of my parents' living room. I thought of Deborah Martinelli, alone in her ransacked house, and willing to ask for help. I thought of her haunted, silvery eyes and the smooth band of flesh between her sweatshirt and the top of her jeans.

"Okay," I said. "All right. Call the police. Don't touch anything. Tell me how to get there."

It took me more than an hour to get to Deborah's place in Carlisle. The highway was littered with the corpses of automobiles with their hoods raised like the mouths of

177

giant birds gaping for food. Victims, I assumed, of drowned engines.

She lived several miles beyond the center of Concord. The road gleamed under my headlights, and I had to keep the windshield wipers on fast speed as the rain continued to fall heavily. I drove past horse farms and woodlands, took a couple of right turns as she had directed me, and found her cedar-and-glass contemporary house snuggled into a pine grove. Her little red Karmann Ghia sat under a carport. A police cruiser was parked behind it. I pulled up beside the cruiser and went to the door.

Deborah answered my knock. She wore tailored yellow slacks and a pale, flowered blouse. Her hair was tied back with a kerchief that matched her slacks. She seemed calm, and even managed one of her sad smiles for me.

"Oh, come in, please. Don't mind the mud. Here, let me take your coat. I'm sorry. The place is such a mess."

I touched her shoulder. "Are you all right?"

"Oh, sure. I'm fine." Again the quick, nervous smile.

She fluttered around me like a mother bird at her nestlings, picking at my trenchcoat, poking at her hair, and flashing her smile on and off. She was in worse shape than I had expected.

I took her arm and guided her into the living room, where a uniformed policeman sat on the sofa, a notebook poised on his knee. The floor on one side of the room lay ankle deep in strewn papers. An old rolltop desk had been pulled away from the wall at an angle. Its drawers hung open and empty like a beggar's pockets.

"Ah, Mr. Coyne, this is Officer Ellis. Mr. Coyne is my lawyer."

I glanced at her and saw no hint of irony on her face. I shook hands with Ellis, who lifted his eyebrows at me and darted his eyes toward Deborah.

"Could I have a cup of tea?" I said to her. She nodded and left the room. I sat on the sofa beside the policeman.

"Thanks," said Ellis after she was gone. "The lady is none too coherent. Kept telling me how her father had been killed, how the same guy was after her now. You're her lawyer, maybe you can make some sense of this for me."

"She's been through a lot," I said, deciding not to contradict Deborah's designation of me as her attorney. I filled Ellis in, and then he summarized for me what he had found. The big desk in the living room and a smaller writing desk in Deborah's bedroom seemed to be the only things that had been rifled. Deborah had not been able to find anything missing in the house. "The guy evidently was looking for something," concluded Ellis. "From what you told me, a good bet is that stamp."

"Which he didn't find," I finished. "Which means that he could be back. For her."

Ellis cocked his head. "A little farfetched, don't you think?"

"No. Two men have already been killed for that stamp."

"That's a theory," said Ellis, "which, from what you've said, the police don't buy."

"The lady needs protection."

He shrugged. "I'll talk with the Chief. Remember, Mr. Coyne, this is Carlisle. We're a pretty quiet little town. We have our share of housebreaks, beered-up teenagers smashing mailboxes, normal number of driving-under-the-influence cases. But damn few assaults. It's a peaceful little community, all in all."

"This lady is in danger."

"Like I say, I'll talk to the Chief."

Ellis went outside, I assumed to use the car radio. As soon as he had left the room, Deborah returned. She set a big mug of tea

180

on the coffee table in front of me and perched on the edge of a straight-backed chair.

"They're not going to do anything, are they?"

I shook my head. "Probably not."

"You know," she said, fixing me with her silvery eyes, "I'm considered quite competent in the business community. Aggressive, even. I hold my own with the men. I've never used the pretty little helpless girl routine to get my way. I play by the rules. I don't bat my eyelashes and let the tears well up in my eyes and say, 'Oh, my, you're so strong.' I want to succeed. And when I do, I don't want anybody to say it's because I'm a lady, because I have some kind of an edge."

I nodded and slurped from the mug of tea.

"But this," she continued, "this makes me feel helpless. Out of control. I figured I was doing okay. I mean, considering that my father was murdered, I was doing pretty damn good. But now – now, I've got to admit it. I'm scared."

"That's reasonable. That's okay. You should be scared."

"It's not being scared that bothers me. It's not being in control. Waiting for someone to come after me."

"Look," I said, "if the police won't

guarantee you protection, I'll stay here tonight."

I assumed she'd protest. Instead, she said, "Okay."

A couple minutes later Ellis returned, shaking his head. "No dice. Best I could do, we'll have a patrol car drive by once in a while."

"Thanks," I said.

"You hear anything, just call the station," he said to Deborah. "Anything at all. Don't hesitate. Like I said, there'll be a car in the area. We can be here in a minute or two."

She nodded.

"Well, I guess that's it, then. You find anything missing, be sure to let us know."

"Sure," said Deborah. She walked to the door with him, closed it behind him, then came back to the living room. She went to the jumble of papers on the floor and sat down. I knelt beside her.

"I'll help," I said.

She turned to look at me. "You know," she said, "you really shouldn't listen to what all those people are saying."

"What do you mean?"

"You're really not such a bad guy. For a lawyer."

"Oh."

Her hand came up and touched my cheek.

Her kiss was cool and soft on the corner of my mouth. I didn't move.

She leaned back, her fingers still on my face, and grinned.

"What was that for?"

"I felt like it. Should I apologize?"

"Nope. Want to do it again?"

"Uh-uh."

She sat back on her heels and began to gather up the papers that lay scattered around her on the floor. I moved back to the sofa and picked up my mug of tea, which I found to be still warm. I held it in both my hands, my elbows on my knees, and watched Deborah scoop up the papers and arrange them on her desk. She moved with economical grace, stooping and stretching, and I enjoyed looking at her. Soon the papers stood in neat piles on the desktop. Then she turned to face me.

"You really don't have to stay. I'll be fine. The police will be around in their car."

I shrugged. "It's up to you."

"I'm okay now." She touched the stacks of papers on the desk, tapping their edges to neaten them. "I can get these organized tomorrow."

"Anything missing?"

"I can't tell for sure. I don't think so."

"Maybe whoever it was wasn't looking for

the stamp at all," I said. "Maybe he was looking for something in the papers."

"You mean something about the stamp?"

"Could be. You know, a letter, an insurance policy, a document of authentication."

"Well, he didn't find anything like that," she said, "because I don't have anything like that."

I stood up. "Guess I'll go, now," I said, "if you're sure you're going to be all right."

"You can have a drink before you go."

"Well, okay," I said. "You twisted my arm."

"If you don't mind," she said, "I'd like to change first. I've still got my work clothes on. I'll be right back."

She returned a few minutes later wrapped in a big, red terrycloth bathrobe. Her hair hung loose. Bare feet peeped from under the full-length robe.

"Now," she said, "what would you like?"

"What I'd really like is popcorn."

She smiled. "Really?"

"Really. Popcorn and Coke is what I want."

"I've got Pepsi. That okay?"

I nodded. "And a cigarette," I added.

"Outside."

"I remember."

The rain had let up. A soft mist drifted through the lights outside Deborah's house. The big pine trees dripped steadily. The air smelled of decay. A little breeze had sprung up, the forerunner of the cold front which would move in behind the storm. It promised winter.

I stood on the little porch smoking until the chilly night air drove me back inside. Deborah called from the kitchen, "Almost ready. Why don't you put on a record?"

We ate popcorn, drank Pepsi-Cola, and listened to Stan Getz, and we didn't talk much. The silence felt comfortable. Deborah curled in one corner of the sofa wrapped in her big red robe with her feet tucked under her. I slipped off my shoes and put my feet up on the coffee table. The big bowl on the cushion between us emptied quickly.

When the records ended, Deborah went to the stereo and knelt in front of it. "Let's hear the other sides," she said. Then, with her back still toward me, she said, "You know about me. But I don't know anything about you. I don't even know if you're married."

"I'm not."

The Getz saxophone filled Deborah's living room with sweet, sad sounds. She curled back into the sofa again. Her pewter

185

eyes regarded me solemnly. "You seem like the sort of man who would be married."

I nodded. "I seem that way to me, too. I was married. Eleven years. It ended one day."

"I'm sorry."

"I was sorry for a long time, too."

"What happened?"

I waved my hand. "One of those things."

"It's painful to you."

"No." I picked at a couple of half-popped kernels in the bottom of the bowl. "No, it's not painful. Do you really want to hear about it?"

"Yes."

"Okay." I sank back into the cushions of the sofa and stared up at the ceiling. "I met Gloria my first year of law school. That was in the early sixties. I used to hang around the Federal courthouse in New Haven. There were lots of interesting civil liberties cases in those days, if you remember. That's what I wanted to do then. First Amendment stuff. The great Constitutional issues. Making history before the Supreme Court. Anyhow, I met this young photographer. She worked for a New Haven paper, and on the side did yearbook portraits for schools, weddings, free-lance stuff for magazines. One day she asked if I'd mind if she photographed me.

She was working on a proposal for *Life* magazine. The faces of young America on the make, something like that. She said I had the prototypical three-piece-suit face. I told her that wasn't very flattering. But she had a great pair of legs and an infectious laugh. Turned out she had no interest whatsoever in photographing me. She just wanted to meet me."

"A three-piece-suit face," repeated Deborah, smiling. "You still have one of those."

"Thanks," I said. "I'm not exactly young America on the make any more, though. We hit it off, Gloria and I. I thought she was the most unusual woman I'd ever met. Totally uninhibited. Great laugh. And she really had talent. We decided not to get married while I was in school. We vowed to keep our careers and our relationship separated. See," I said, "part of what I loved about Gloria was her talent and her independence. We lived together, off and on, for two years. This was way before that was an acceptable thing to do. Gloria didn't care. It was her idea. And we got married the day after I got my degree from Yale."

"Then it changed," said Deborah.

"Yes. Oh, it was very gradual. Not even noticeable, at first. We got a house in

Wellesley, joined the country club, had a couple of kids. She didn't do much photography, except our own family. Always taking pictures of the boys. She became absorbed in the boys and the house. Our conversations grew narrower and narrower. The price of pork chops, the evils of house dust, the relative merits of nursery schools, crab grass, laundry detergent."

I looked at Deborah. Her arms were folded across her knees. Her chin rested on her hands, and she was studying me with her gray eyes.

"You got bored with her," she said.

I nodded. "Yes. One day I realized it. Our marriage was boring. She had changed. She was dull. The laughter was gone."

"So you dumped her."

"That's not..."

Deborah's eyes narrowed. "No, I understand. Gloria was stuck raising the kids, taking care of the house, and you went out into the world every day. What the hell did you expect?"

I nodded. "Sure. That's what I figured, too. I begged her to go back to work. I told her we'd get a maid. The kids were in school. Hell, I pleaded with her to get out of the house. I figured that's what she wanted. But see, it wasn't like that. It wasn't what she wanted at all. It had gone too far, I guess. She *wanted* to talk about pork chops and house dust. It's all that interested her. Everything I had loved about her was dying. There was only one way to save her."

"Really magnanimous. You dumped her to save her. Some rationalization!"

"I liberated her," I said.

"Humph!" snorted Deborah. "Then what?"

"It worked. You've got to understand something. I had the ideal marriage, by conventional standards. A dutiful wife, great cook, wonderful mother. She kept her figure, made love whenever I wanted – at least pretended enthusiasm for it – good hostess, charmed my clients, nice backhand. No bad habits. Never nagged me, never questioned my comings and goings. But it saddened me, and I couldn't allow her to turn into a Stepford wife, a mindless servant to what she thought were my wishes and needs. Hell, she wouldn't even contest the divorce. 'If that's what you want,' she said."

"Then what happened?"

"Then I wasn't around any more to give her life any meaning. She had to find it herself. She went through a bad few months. Kept calling me. But eventually she started taking pictures again. And three years after our divorce, to the day, she called me up and asked me out to dinner. I went. She was bubbling. Had a contract from some magazine to do a photographic series on historic homes in Newport. We had champagne. She said to me, 'You forced me to be free. Thank you.' She was her old self again."

"Forced to be free," said Deborah. "Nice for you, it seems to me."

I shook my head. "No. Not nice for me. Not at all. Like you said earlier, I'm the sort of man who should be married. My life was a lot better – a lot richer – when I was married. It was Gloria, I think, who was the sort of woman who shouldn't be married."

"Why haven't you remarried, then?"

"I think," I said, "what I actually am, is the sort of man who should be married to Gloria. But Gloria's not the sort of woman who should be married at all. Or at least, not to me."

Deborah stared at me with her chin perched atop her knees. Her hair fell forward, framing her face, so that she reminded me of an owl. "That's either a very tragic story," she said, shaking her head slowly, "or else it's a great big rationalization."

I shrugged.

"So you still love her, then."

"From afar. In the abstract. Yes, I suppose so."

"And the two boys," she said. "Where do they fit in?" Her eyes narrowed. "If you had to do it again, would you have children?"

I smiled at her. "Sure. But not the same ones."

She frowned.

"That was a joke."

Deborah turned her face so that her cheek rested on her forearm. "Very funny." She closed her eyes.

I stretched and stood up. "Well," I said. "It's late. Tomorrow's a work day. I'll be leaving."

"You might as well stay," she said. "I can make up the couch," she added quickly. "It pulls out. It's quite comfortable."

I reached to touch her shoulder, but she stood up and moved away from me. "I hope you don't misunderstand."

"Oh, no. I understand. The couch will be fine."

We each took an end of the heavy coffee table and moved it aside. Then I pulled out the fold-away bed while Deborah went for sheets and blankets. We made up the bed together like a comfortably married couple, stretching the sheets between us, tucking them under, and smoothing two blankets on top. She produced a pillow and laid a folded afghan across the foot of the bed.

"Your bathroom is off the kitchen. There's a new toothbrush and clean towels. If there's anything else you need . . ." She sounded like the girl behind the counter at a Holiday Inn.

"That sounds fine," I said.

"What time do you get up in the morning?"

"Earlier than I want to," I said. "I'll wake up around five. I used to be able to sleep. No more. I don't need an alarm."

"Well, okay, then. I'll make some breakfast for you. Good night." She reached up on tiptoes and kissed my cheek lightly. Then she disappeared behind a door down a short hallway.

I wandered outside for the day's last cigarette. The carpet of pine needles was soft and damp underfoot. Up through the canopy of pines I could see the clouds skidding across the moonlit sky. The wind rustled high in the trees. I shivered. If the wind died, there would be a frost, the first of the season. The storm had swept summer away.

I was edgy. The melancholy of a stormy Sunday evening still lingered in the fuzzy part of my consciousness, and the evil that had invaded Deborah's house mixed with it to produce a lump of malaise in my chest. I looked back at the house. Lights glowed warm and orange through the windows of the living room.

I stamped out my cigarette and went back inside. I checked the locks on both the front and back doors and found the broken pane of glass that had allowed the invader to get in. Nothing I could do about that. If he wanted to come back, he'd get in. I hoped that my car in the driveway would deter him if he decided to return that night.

There was no sound from the direction of Deborah's bedroom. I hoped she felt secure. I wished I did. I remembered once again the little black hole at the base of Albert Dopplinger's skull, and the rusty brown stain on Francis Shaughnessey's carpet, and the taste of chloroform in my mouth. I found Deborah's liquor supply in a kitchen cabinet and poured myself half a tumbler of Jim Beam. I brought it into the living room and turned the stereo on low. I sipped bourbon and listened to Stan Getz and Astrud Gilberto's unforgettable rendering of "The Girl from Ipanema." The upbeat bossa nova failed to raise my spirits.

Deborah had left two big, fluffy bath towels and a new toothbrush still wrapped in cellophane in the bathroom for me. I showered quickly and sipped the last of my bourbon while I toweled myself dry. Then I laid my clothes as neatly as I could over a chair, turned out all the lights, and crawled naked into my bed.

It was more comfortable than I'd expected, and sleep came quickly. It seemed like only minutes, but it had been perhaps an hour when I sensed a presence in the room with me. Immediately my nerves went on alert. I lay still and forced my breathing to remain slow and regular. I lifted my eyelids a millimeter. A figure stood beside my bed, and it took me just an instant to realize it was Deborah. I let my eyelids fall shut again.

I felt her fingers on my face, a tentative touch, as if she were testing the feel of my skin. Her hand lingered there for a moment, lightly, absent-mindedly tracing the line from my cheekbone along my jaw. Then it moved away. I could smell her fragrance, clean and soapy.

Then her hand grasped my shoulder, none too gently.

"Hey," she said. "Hey, Coyne. You awake?"

I opened my eyes to look at her. She was standing beside my bed staring down at me. She wore a shapeless, pale-colored nightgown. Her hair hung loose around her face.

I yawned ostentatiously. "Funny thing," I said. "Sleep seems to be eluding me."

She sat beside me, her rump solid and warm against my shoulder. "Listen," she said. "You wanna hold me a little while?"

"Sure. Okay," I said.

Afterward, she curled herself into a little fetal ball and backed tightly against the front of me. I lay on my side, my face in her hair and my arm around her, snuggling her against me. She held my wrist in both of her hands. Her nightgown had ridden up over her hips, and her skin was warm and soft and alive where it touched mine. Her body rocked gently with the rhythms of her sleep. And then I slept, too.

I awakened in time to watch the blackness through the windows fade into brightening shades of gray. Deborah still slept against me. I shifted cautiously until I was able to extricate my arm from where she held it against her breast. She groaned and rolled onto her stomach. I slid out from the bed and pulled the blankets up over her. Then I took a long shower.

When I got out, she was still sleeping. I dressed quickly in the dim, predawn light of the room. I found a pencil and some blank paper in her rolltop desk. I wrote her several notes. I tore each of them up. They sounded like explanations, or apologies, which wasn't what I intended, or else like love notes. I didn't intend that, either. So I left no note at all.

I paused beside the bed and reached down to smooth her hair. Then I went to my car and drove to Boston. It was Monday. I had work to do.

Chapter 10

I called Charlie McDevitt in the middle of the morning to make a date for lunch. His choice of restaurants. We agreed to meet at the Common by the subway entrance.

Then I called Deborah's office.

"Colonial Properties of Concord. This is Darlene. May I help you?"

I asked for Ms. Martinelli, emphasizing the *miz*.

"Who may I say is calling?"

"You may say it's Brady Coyne."

"One moment, please."

I heard myself being put on hold. Then my ear was assaulted with elevator music. The Ray Coniff chorus, it sounded like, performing their own distinctive rendition of a medley of Beatles tunes. "I Wanna Hold Your Hand," in waltz time. A neat segue into an arrangement of "Eleanor Rigby" that would have done Lawrence Welk proud.

Darlene came back on the phone, interrupting a lullaby version of "Tax Man." "Deborah can't come to the phone right now. May I have her return your call? Or would you care to leave a message?"

"Tell her she should get a Stan Getz tape if she's going to make people listen to music when they're on hold," I said. "And just tell her I called."

"How do you spell that, please?"

"C-o-y-n-e."

"No, the other name."

"Oh, G-e-t-z. Stan Getz. Tenor sax. You never heard of Stan Getz?"

"I'll give her your message, Mr. Coyne."

I reminded myself to congratulate Deborah on the efficiency of her secretary. Humorless, but efficient. Darlene impressed me as one of those women who would sniff and wrinkle her chin if a man winked at her.

I climbed out of the murk of the subway landing into the brilliant October noon sunshine. Tremont Street swarmed with secretaries and executives hurrying to the Union Oyster House and Jake Wirth's for lunch. The young matrons of summer, tugging their ice-cream-dirty toddlers toward the swan boats, had deserted the Common. In their place milled a mix of elderly ladies bearing shopping bags like fragile trophies, college students lolling on the benches, their faces turned to the sun, and old men feeding popcorn to the pigeons. I blinked a couple of times, looked around, and finally located Charlie. He was standing, deep in conversation with a younger man who was keeping watch over a square metal pushcart, at the point where the paths that intersect the Common converge. A sign on the pushcart promised KING SIZE FRANKS AND KRAUT: 75 ¢.

Charlie saw me and waved me over.

"Brady Coyne," he said when I was standing beside him, "Johnny Pilarski."

Pilarski gave me a lopsided grin from the depths of his thick, black beard and shoved out his hand. He wore sunglasses and the reflector lenses that the state troopers who patrol the Mass Pike favor. I saw the image of myself mirrored in each lens.

"Nice to meetcha, Mr. Coyne," said Pilarski, who then returned his attention to Charlie. "Fifty percent suits me, Mr. Mac. I'm satisfied with fifty percent. It covers it, you know?"

Charlie was shaking his head and smiling. "You take what you can get in this world, Johnny."

Pilarski held up his hand. "No. You take what you deserve. No more, no less."

Charlie turned to me. "We have this argument all the time."

"I always win," grinned Pilarski.

"Dumb-ass Polack," said Charlie. "Hell with it. Be poor. I don't give a shit."

"Rather make an honest buck," said Pilarski, with a sly emphasis on the word *honest*. "You know?"

"Nobody likes lawyers," moaned Charlie. "What is it – ninety percent of all Washington politicians are lawyers? Ever since Watergate. Goddam Nixon is a lawyer. How the hell you going to fight that? Listen. Mr. Coyne here is a lawyer, you know."

"I figured," chuckled Pilarski. "About the only friends lawyers have are other lawyers, huh? Hey, shit, it's okay. You guys do run the world. You want to be liked, too? I'll sell my hot dogs, thank you. I clear thirty-seven cents on every dog I sell. Thirty-seven *honest* pennies."

Charlie shrugged. He turned to me. "This guy's impossible. Well. You ready for some lunch?"

"Sure. Where you taking me?"

"We're here, my man."

Charlie and I took our dogs and kraut to a bench from which we could look up at the golden dome of the State House. I told Charlie the story of the Dutch Blue Error. He picked stray strands of sauerkraut off the front of his jacket and listened intently.

"So," I concluded, "somebody wants that stamp badly enough to kill two men for it. And I'm afraid Deborah is next on his list. And, just for spice, Zerk is a suspect."

"You sleeping with her?"

"What makes you ask that?"

Charlie burped loudly. "I thought so."

"Well, what do you think?"

"What did you think of Johnny Pilarski?"

I shrugged. "Seems like a nice enough guy."

"He's only got one foot, you know."

"No. I couldn't tell."

"And no eyes."

"He's blind?"

"Most people without any eyes are blind, Counselor. Claymore mine. He's from my old neighborhood in Southie. He was a cocky little snot-nose punk when I went off to college. Best damn little ten-year-old basketball player you ever saw, though. For a white kid, anyway. Dribble through his legs, behind his back. Actually had a jump shot. How many ten-year-old kids do you know who can shoot jumpers? Anyhow, he quit school his senior year and joined up, went to Vietnam, and was back in a week, minus one foot and two eyes. His mother called me. Figured I had a lot of pull with the government – which, as you know, I don't

– and would be able to get him a hundred-percent disability. Of course I *could* do that. He could do that himself. Hell. Even *you* could do that. But you heard him back there. He won't take it. He applied for fifty percent. He insists he's only fifty percent disabled. He says lots of guys lost both legs, or both hands, or their balls, or their sanity. Lots came home in bags. They're the ones who should get the hundred percent, so says Johnny."

"He doesn't think of himself as disabled."

"Exactly. See, it's a matter of perspective. Depends on how you look at it."

I nodded. "That's interesting, and I'm glad to have met the man, and now I forgive you for the lunch. But I was asking you about my little problem. Granted, I'd rather have my problem than Johnny's but still . . ."

"But, see, that's my point. He ain't what he seems to be. You didn't know he was blind. After you get to know him for a while, you figure it out. And once you know it, you can tell by watching him – little ways he has with his hands, how his head turns so that those reflector shades he wears always look right at you. And once you know it, you can never go back to seeing him the other way. Seems to me that's your problem, too."

"Things not being what they seem, you mean."

"Yeah. And being able to see things differently. Knowing that one thing – like Johnny Pilarski being blind – that changes everything else. See, old buddy, you've never been a prosecutor. Your skills are rusty. Hell, I think they're so corroded they've seized up. You *believe* people. But that's your problem. You can't believe people. Because someone's always lying. A prosecutor's got to figure there's a lie somewhere."

I stared at the State House dome. "Okay," I said, "somebody's lying. Now what?"

"Simple," said Charlie. "You've got to go through everybody, one at a time. Assume each one's telling a lie. Ask yourself: What is the lie? If it's a lie, what might the truth be? And why is that person lying?" He stared at me. "See? It's tedious. But it's the way."

I shook my head. "Give me a for instance."

"Okay. For instance, the lady. Deborah. Who you're sleeping with. Suppose she's telling a lie. What lie could she be telling you – besides she loves your body?"

"She never said that," I said. I thought for a minute. "She said she doesn't know where the stamp is. That could be a lie."

"And the truth . . ."

"One truth might be that she's got the stamp. Or she at least knows where it is. Which amounts to the same thing."

"And," persisted Charlie, "why might she tell that lie?"

"Damned if I know," I said. "but it's a very interesting question."

"See?" said Charlie. "See how it works?"

"Gets you thinking, I see that," I said. "But you know, this game isn't much fun."

"You've just been away from the hurly-burly too long," he said. "Stop feeling sorry for yourself."

"I *wanna* feel sorry for myself. I want *you* to feel sorry for me."

"Johnny Pilarski tells a story he heard when he was in the hospital getting fitted for a plastic foot. You want to hear it?"

"I think I'm going to anyway," I said.

"Right," said Charlie. He leaned back against the bench and put his right ankle across his left thigh and clasped his neck. "Once upon a time," he began, "there was a man who had everything. That once upon a time gives it away, don't you think? I mean you know there's a fairy tale coming at you. Anyway, this guy had piles of money, a job he loved, the best of health, a gorgeous wife who adored him, two smart children, a mansion in the country, a Mercedes all paid up.

"On the way to work one morning the Mercedes threw a rod. The man stood beside his car, which he loved, looked to the sky, and said, 'Why me, God?'

"By the time he got to work, the coffee pot was empty, his shirt was dirty, and his secretary was out sick. His boss was waiting for him in his office.

"'We're reorganizing,' said the boss. 'You're through. Clean out your desk.'

"'Why me, God?' begged the man.

"When he got home, the house was empty. On the kitchen table he found a note from his wife. 'I'm leaving you,' it said. 'I'm taking the children. I'm taking the money from the bank accounts. My lawyer will contact you.'

"The man's eyes filled with tears, for he loved his wife and he loved his children and he loved his bank accounts. 'Why me, God?' he cried.

"He stumbled out of the house, sobbing. He wandered around the grounds that he loved. All he had left was his mansion. Suddenly the sky darkened, thunder boomed, and a great bolt of lightning stabbed down from the black clouds. The man heard a huge explosion behind him. He turned in time to see his house burst into flames.

Within minutes it was reduced to a heap of smoldering rubble. The man sat on the grass and buried his face in his hands. Then he raised both arms to the heavens and wailed, 'Why me, God?'

"The clouds suddenly parted and a strange shaft of golden light shone down on the man's face. He heard a deep, unearthly voice rumble from above: 'I don't know, man,' said the voice. 'I guess you just kinda piss me off.' "

Charlie sat forward and smiled at me. "They told that in the VA hospital, these guys with no legs and no faces. According to Johnny, it's exactly what they all believed. That summed up their theology."

"Pretty fundamental theology," I said. "Calvinist, really."

"Johnny says it kept them going. Whenever any one of them bitched to a nurse, or complained about his pain, or criticized the food, someone would yell at him, 'Why me, God?' and another guy would answer, 'I dunno, man. I guess you just piss me off.' Johnny says you had to laugh."

"You're telling me I shouldn't be feeling sorry for myself," I said. "Compared to those guys in the hospital."

"Compared to the guy in the story, maybe.

Whatever. I just thought you'd enjoy the story."

"I guess I should get to work."

"Or not," said Charlie. "God doesn't give a shit."

"Think I'll get to work," I said.

Chapter 11

When I returned to my office from my hot dog and sauerkraut lunch, I found Zerk pounding furiously at his typewriter. His jacket hung over the back of his chair, his cuffs were rolled halfway up his forearms, and his tie was pulled loose from his collar. The IBM clattered angrily under his fingers. He didn't look up when I went over to stand beside him.

I waited for a pause in the rhythm of his typing. He came to the end of a sheet. His machine fell suddenly silent. He reached up with both hands and yanked the paper out of his machine.

"Any calls?" I said.

"None for you."

He rolled a fresh sheet of paper into the typewriter and ostentatiously ran his finger along the edited manuscript from which he was copying.

"Something I should know about?"

"Nope."

"Why do I think you're lying to me?"

Zerk swiveled around and glared up at me. "Same reason the fat man does, maybe."

"The fat man?"

"The cop."

"Oh. Stone."

"Yeah. Stone."

"Stone was here?"

"Stone called me. Stone knows I killed those two guys. Stone's gonna get me. Stone's a tough guy. Stone's smart and patient. Stone's gonna get his lungs ripped out."

"You can't let him get to you, Zerk. He's trying to make you blow your cool."

"Right. I figured that out." He pushed himself away from his desk and pounded his thighs with his fists. "He is, too, the son of a bitch. Makes it seem personal."

"You want a cup of coffee?"

"I want a drink. I wanna smoke some dope. I wanna bust up a face."

"So let's go get a drink."

"I got work to do. Leave me alone."

"Were there any other calls?"

"Like from a lady?"

I shrugged.

"No. I told you. No calls for you."

He wheeled himself back to his desk, fiddled with the typewriter for a minute, then his fingers began to fire staccato bursts on the machine. I went into my office and picked up the telephone.

Darlene informed me that Deborah was out with a client, she didn't know when she'd be back, yes, she had delivered my earlier messages, and she would tell Deborah that Mr. Coyne had called again.

I placed a yellow legal pad on the desk in front of me and with pencil divided it vertically into four columns. I wrote headings at the top of each column. The lie. Reason for the lie. The truth. Then I filled in the first column with all the relevant names, leaving plenty of space between them. I figured each person could have contributed several lies, each of which would suggest several alternative truths, and each of which might have several possible motivations. Ollie Weston was the first name on my list. His first lie I phrased simply as "Dutch Blue Error." I didn't know what the lie might be, but I realized that until I knew more about the stamp I wouldn't be able to imagine the lie.

I opened the Yellow Pages to PHILATELY, and found nothing. I tried STAMPS, and found what I wanted under STAMPS FOR COLLECTORS. I learned that in the city of Boston several dozen stamp dealers plied their trade, and a great many of them had their offices on Bromfield Street. I copied down some addresses.

Zerk didn't look up, nor did the tempo of his typing change, when I left my office.

Bromfield Street is a narrow little one-way street, wide enough only for a single automobile to pass. It cuts across from Tremont Street to Washington Street near the Boston Common, right opposite the Granary Burial Ground, a two-minute walk from where Charlie and I had eaten our hot dogs an hour earlier.

I selected one of those office buildings randomly and walked into the dark lobby. Under a framed glass panel a directory listed three stamp dealers. Two were located on the second floor. I found no elevator, so I climbed the stairs.

I arrived at the office of Morris Graustein. His name was hand-printed on an index card taped to his door. He had a thick bush of curly white hair, watery blue eyes, and yellow teeth. He wore a tattered blue cardigan sweater over a faded plaid shirt. His tiny office contained a large wooden desk, several head-high metal file cabinets, a couple of cardboard boxes piled on top of each other in a corner, and a single pigeon-stained window which looked fuzzily onto the building across the street.

Morris Graustein sat at his paper-strewn desk sipping from a mug and staring at the telephone. When I entered the room he said, "Come in, sir, come in. Nice day, eh? Are you buying or selling today?" Graustein pronounced it "buy-ink or sell-ink."

He looked up at me. When he smiled, a thousand wrinkles spread across his face as if a strong wind had sprung up suddenly over a placid body of water. "Or maybe you want to buy a little starter outfit for your nephew, eh?" He squinted as if he could see into my intentions. "Aha, yes. I have got it. You have a shoebox full of United States first-day covers you want to sell because you have collected them for twenty years and now it is time to put the children into college. Am I right, sir?"

I laughed. "I'm not a philatelist. You're right. My name is Coyne, I'm an attorney, and I need some information about a rare stamp."

"Coyne." The breeze blew across Graustein's face again. "You should be a numismatist, Mr. Coyne. Your first name, it isn't Bill, is it, sir?"

I smiled and shook my head. "No. It's Brady."

"Well," he continued, "there just happens to be the smallest lull in my business at this

212

moment, and you just happen to be talking with a man who knows all about rare stamps, sir." He glanced again at his telephone. "So. Do you want to know about a particular rare stamp? Or rare stamps in general? How may I help you, Mr. Coyne?"

"A particular one. It's called the Dutch Blue Error. Are you familiar with it?"

He ran his fingers through his thick tangle of white hair. "Everybody is familiar with the blue 1852 Netherlands fifteen-cent. I cannot tell you how to buy it, sir. But I can tell you many things about it." He bent over and rummaged in a drawer in his desk. In a moment he produced a tattered old magazine, which he flipped through and then spread out on the desktop in front of me. "The official story is in here. You can read it. But it is not the whole story, sir."

"What do you mean?"

"Let me ask you a question, sir," said Graustein.

"What's my interest in the stamp, right?"

He nodded.

"I'm inquiring for a client."

He lifted his eyebrows.

"That's all I can tell you," I said.

"Does your client want to buy the Dutch Blue Error?"

I smiled and shrugged.

"Because if he does, I cannot help you. However, if he desires to sell it . . ."

"Yes?"

"If he wants to sell it – if your client owns the Dutch Blue Error – I would like to have the opportunity to buy it from him. Will you tell him that for me, sir? You might not think so, but I *could* buy that stamp."

"My client," I said carefully, "wants neither to buy nor to sell the Dutch Blue Error. Believe me. I just want to learn about it. I just need the information."

Graustein sighed. "Yes. Well, have it that way, then. All right. Briefly. The Blue Error, it is assumed, was originally one of a single sheet of the fifteen-cent orange issue. The plate was probably incorrectly inked. It may have been the first sheet printed, and the printer realized his mistake after the first sheet was produced. No one knows. There are many ways such errors can be made. At any rate, the stamps probably did not circulate, except for the Blue Error of which you inquire. None of the others, if there was an entire sheet, has ever turned up, sir. It has been assumed for many years that the other blue errors – if there were others – were destroyed by the printer. Perhaps they have simply disappeared. Once that assumption became widely accepted, once it seemed

214

probable that there were no other blue errors, the value of that one stamp increased rapidly. Of course, it is possible – not likely, I should say, sir, but possible – that there are others yet to be found."

Graustein told me of the stamp's discovery by a Dutch boy in 1885, his sale of it to a dealer, and the periodic exchanges of the stamp among European dealers. "Each of these sales is documented," he said. "Right up to the last one."

"When was that?"

"That was 1967, at an auction in Paris."

"And the stamp hasn't been sold since then?"

"No."

"Could it be sold privately?"

"Only in violation of the tax laws of every civilized nation on earth, sir," said Graustein. "No. It is assumed that the 1967 buyer still owns the Dutch Blue Error."

"Who," I asked hesitantly, "was that buyer?"

He shrugged. "I do not know."

"You don't?"

"No. It is a mystery. The man who did know is dead."

"Dead?" I elevated my eyebrows to encourage him.

"Yes. The agent. The sale, we assume, was

made to an American. Perhaps an individual, more likely a corporation or a conglomerate. Conceivably even a museum, although one would assume they would want to show the stamp. In any case, whoever bought it used a purchaser. An agent, a Frenchman, who acted on behalf of the buyer. This is quite common among wealthy collectors, sir. They have agents in the major cities with the authority and the access to funds to make purchases. In any case, a French agent purchased the Blue Error in April of 1967."

"He has since died, you say."

Graustein's faded blue eyes stared at me. "He died within twenty-four hours of the transaction. He was found in the swimming pool of the hotel in San Juan, Puerto Rico, with a broken neck. Suicide, sir. He jumped from the balcony outside the building into the pool. Eight floors down."

I took out a Winston and tapped it on the top of his desk.

"Oh, please, sir. Do not smoke in here."

"Sorry," I said, sticking the cigarette back into the pack.

"I do not stock a great number of stamps. But those I have are very valuable. The smoke is not good for them. And I do fear fire, sir."

"I understand." I returned the pack to my

pocket. "So this French agent was the last one to have the stamp."

"It is believed that he bought the stamp and delivered it to his client in Puerto Rico before he jumped from the balcony. The trail of the Dutch Blue Error ends there, sir. In 1967 in San Juan with the suicide of the French agent."

My mind whirled with half-formed thoughts.

"Of course," continued Graustein, "there are stories. Now and then a Dutch Blue Error story will make the rounds. The latest story is that one of Fidel Castro's henchmen duped the French agent out of the stamp, and when the Frenchman realized what had been done to him, he took his own life so that he would not have to face his client."

"What do *you* think, Mr. Graustein?"

"Me?" He looked surprised. "I do not know, sir. There was an earlier story that makes about as much sense."

I smiled and waited.

Graustein rested his forearms on his desktop and leaned toward me. "The Dutch Blue Error has always been owned by Europeans. In 1934 it was purchased from an Englishman by a Parisian. Monsieur Ouelette. When Paris was occupied, so the story goes, Ouelette bought his and his family's passage to Switzerland from a Nazi officer. The Dutch Blue Error was the price of his liberty. According to the tale, a Citroën registered to a Monsieur Ouelette drove off a mountain a few miles short of the Swiss border."

I shook my head. I thought of Francis Shaughnessey and Albert Dopplinger. A lot of dead men lay strewn in the wake of the Dutch Blue Error.

"When the 1967 transaction was made," he continued, "the agent who sold it had all the right papers. He claimed to be acting on behalf of a Mr. Ouelette." Graustein shrugged. "Ouelette is not an uncommon name. So who knows whether it is a true story or not? But that is not the interesting thing, sir."

"The interesting thing?"

"Yes. The interesting thing is this. If you believe the story, the Nazis intended to create several duplicates of the Blue Error."

"Duplicates!" Scenarios abounded. "Why would they want to do that?"

"Possibly simply to make money. The Nazis, as you remember, were very interested in owning valuable things. Or else, as a part of their grand plan, they intended to devalue all things not owned by the Germans." He pronounced it "Chermans."

"I don't understand," I said.

"If good forgeries of the Dutch Blue Error began to turn up, people would become increasingly cautious about buying other rare stamps. That would be natural, do you see, sir? It would be considered a poor investment. The market would become depressed. Conceivably at that point, agents of the German government would begin to buy up the rare stamps of the world, just as they had confiscated and hoarded the contents of the great museums and private collections of Europe." Graustein shrugged again. "It is just a story. Since the Nazis lost the war, I suppose we will never know."

"I thought forgeries were easy to detect."

"That is very complicated, sir," he said. He turned his head around to stare at the clock on the wall behind him. It was 4:25. "Very complicated to explain about forgeries," he repeated.

"Mr. Graustein, suppose I buy you a beer?"

"A nice glass of German beer. Yes, that would be fine, sir," said Graustein, smiling as if he hadn't thought of it. "I even know a little place."

He fumbled with the several locks on his door and led me down the stairs and out onto Bromfield Street. We turned left, and at the end of the alley emerged onto Washington Street. We had entered what is universally known as Boston's Combat Zone. The City Fathers, in their infinite wisdom, have designated that stretch of Washington Street a kind of legal no-man's land, a free-fire area, where porno film operators, topless dancers, prostitutes, and pimps can all ply their dubious trades more or less free of official interference, and visiting salesmen and commuting executives can buy watered-down drinks for five bucks, provided they'll do the same for the bar girls who sit beside them, and by asking the right questions they can also invest in a case of herpes to bring home to their wives.

In the evening, loud music spills out onto the streets, hookers stroll in pairs and threesomes, cars creep slowly along the streets, and old men urinate in the alleys against the brick walls. A few years ago, a Harvard football player was stabbed to death in a Combat Zone bar. He and some of his teammates had gone to celebrate their season, which had ended with a glorious victory over Yale. He was a linebacker, a senior who had played the last game of his career that afternoon. A pre-med student, the papers said.

No one ever figured out who stabbed the

kid, or why. A cop was quoted as saying that was the risk you took going into the Combat Zone.

But at 4:30 on a bright Monday afternoon in early October, the Combat Zone was enjoying an armistice. The people who walked along the sidewalks barely glanced into the darkened establishments along the way. They seemed to be just passing through, secretaries and bankers and accountant executives on their way home from their State Street offices.

Graustein led me to a tiny bar wedged between a place that displayed photos of big-busted women in advanced states of nudity, and a movie theater whose marguee boasted: ALL X-RATED!!!

I followed Morris Graustein through the door into a narrow, dark barroom. At the far end, a small color television was tuned to an afternoon soap opera, and a thin man in a short-sleeved white shirt leaned against the wall behind the bar, staring at it. When Graustein hopped up onto a stool, the bartender glanced over and lifted his eyebrows. Graustein nodded and smiled. The thin man poured a tall glass of coffee-colored beer from a tap and set it on a cardboard coaster in front of the stamp dealer.

"Thank you, Jimmy," he said. "And you, my friend? Will you have the same?"

"Sure," I said.

Jimmy brought two glasses of the dark brew and whisked away Graustein's first, already empty. "Ah," he said. "The first for the thirst, and the rest for the taste." He lifted it toward me, then raised it to his lips. I imitated him. The beer was strong and creamy and faintly bitter.

"Now, sir," said Graustein, wiping a frothy mustache from his lips with the sleeve of his shirt, "you wanted to know about fraudulent stamps."

I shrugged. "It sounds interesting. And you mentioned the Nazis . . ."

He waved his hand. "Oh, sir, that is only a tale. I do not think that happened."

"In any case."

"Yes. Well, then." Graustein sipped his beer. "There are two kinds of fraudulent stamps, sir. First there are the forgeries. Counterfeits. Like paper money, eh? And as with counterfeit money, knowledgeable people cannot be fooled by forged stamps."

"They can't?"

"Oh, my, no. There are too many ways to detect forgeries. The size, the details of the design, the color and type of ink, the type of paper, the quality and color of the gum, the manufacturing process – all of these are variables, sir, that the expert can examine. Just as with paper money."

"I see," I said. "Forgeries really aren't a problem, then."

"Not with very rare stamps, sir. They are examined too carefully. Sometimes with middle-range stamps we find forgeries. But your concern is the Dutch Blue Error, and no forgery would escape the detection of an expert. It would be an absurd waste of effort to forge such a stamp. Absurd." Graustein shook his head in dismay at the thought.

Jimmy, who had returned to his television program, glanced over and said, "Again, gentlemen?"

"Why, yes, Jimmy. Please," said Graustein.

"You mentioned a second kind of fraud," I said.

"Ah, thank you, Jimmy," he said to the bartender, who replaced our empty glasses with full ones. The philatelist sipped from his glass. "Mmm. Ambrosia. Nectar of the gods. Divine. Wonderful." He pronounced it "vunderful."

"Fakes," said Graustein.

"Huh?"

"The second kind of fraud, sir. Fakes.

These are genuine stamps that are altered to increase their value. A much nastier matter."

I raised my eyebrows over the rim of my glass. Graustein's eyes twinkled in reply.

"The third great pillar of philatelic value, sir," he said. "Condition." Then he frowned. "Of no interest with regard to your Blue Error stamp. The British Guyana black and magenta, of course, which we generally acknowledge to be the single most valuable stamp in the world – it is in perfectly horrible condition. Corners cut off, nasty blob of a postmark. With stamps of this great rarity, these unique stamps, condition is less of a factor than supply and demand. Most especially, of course, demand."

I nodded. Ollie Weston had told me much the same thing.

"On the other hand," he continued, after a long draught from his glass, "there are hundreds of genuinely rare and valuable stamps for which condition is all-important. A very fine mint stamp – well centered, clear, bright color, unhinged, with original gum, perforations nicely torn – that stamp might be worth, let us say, three thousand dollars. That would be a collector's prize. And the same stamp, off center, or color faded by the sun, perhaps creased or with a tiny half-millimeter tear in the corner, or with pulled perforations – actually, sir, with any one of those seemingly minor defects – your same stamp might bring you forty or fifty dollars. If you find someone to buy it. No bargain, sir."

"Yes. I see."

"So, you create a fake from that stamp. You alter it, you repair a crease or a tear or a thin spot, let us say. Or perhaps you erase or fade a heavy cancellation – what we call a 'killer blob.' With care, this can be done with chemicals. Or you can brighten faded color, eliminate a stain, regum the back. There are unscrupulous men who will doctor stamps in such ways to increase their value, do you see? Alas, it is most difficult to detect. Few have the skill and the equipment with which to detect such clever doctoring of stamps."

"Have you ever heard of Albert Dopplinger?" I asked him.

"Ah, poor Albert. I knew Albert, yes."

"Was he considered . . ."

"Oh, my, yes. The best. Better by far than me, sir. And he had all the equipment. The microscopes, the quartz lights, the chemicals. Nobody was better than Albert." Graustein shook his head. "He is dead, you know."

"Yes. He was murdered."

Graustein turned again to stare at me. His eyes were solemn. "Is this why . . .?"

"No," I said, "I told you. I'm an attorney."

"Because I know of no one who would want to murder Albert Dopplinger, sir."

"I'm sure of it," I said. "I have no interest in the murder case. I'm interested in the Dutch Blue Error."

"On the other hand," Graustein continued, as if I had not spoken, "men have been murdered for stamps. Oh, yes."

I raised my eyebrows.

He steepled his fingers in front of his face. "The two-cent Hawaiian Missionary of 1851. There are only fifteen of them in existence. According to the story, they were used by missionaries on their mail back to the mainland. Cheap, unattractive stamps. But valuable to collectors. They are worth perhaps one hundred thousand dollars today, the two-cents. Not as valuable as your Blue Error, sir, but valuable stamps. Worth killing for, some might say. Hm. Shall we have more beer, sir?"

I nodded and gestured to Jimmy, who slid two brimming glasses to us.

"One day, sometime in the eighteen-nineties," continued Graustein, after a long draught on his beer, "I forget the exact year,

226

a gentleman named Gaston Leroux was found murdered in his Paris flat. The police had no clues – no known enemies, no motive, no evidence of theft. There was money still there, gold coins, a diamond watch. But Leroux was a philatelist, and one of the investigators happened to know a bit about stamps. He examined the dead man's collection and determined that there was one stamp missing. Yes, sir. The two-cent Missionary of 1851. So the detective thought that he might have a motive for murder, and his suspicions soon centered on a gentleman named Hector Giroux, a friend of Leroux and himself a collector. The detective befriended the unsuspecting Giroux. They had, after all, a common passion in philately. And one evening Giroux invited the inspector to his flat. The detective turned the conversation to the Missionary stamps, and Giroux was duped into proudly showing off his collection to the detective. It contained one of the two-cents – the precise one, the detective was convinced, that had belonged to the late M. Leroux. The next day Giroux was arrested and interrogated. He was unable to explain satisfactorily how he had acquired the two-cent Missionary. No papers, you see. No authentication, no bill of sale. So he was charged with the murder of Gaston Leroux.

And eventually he confessed. His explanation, which, one imagines, he may have considered a justification, was that he needed the two-cent to complete his collection of Hawaiian Missionaries." Graustein smiled elfishly at me. "Only a true philatelist could sympathize with Hector Giroux, eh?"

I returned his smile. "I suppose you're right," I said. "But, as I said, I am only interested in the Dutch Blue Error."

"And you want to know about fakes and forgeries. And you knew Albert." Graustein nodded his head up and down several times. Then he turned to grin at me. "Well, maybe you will find the man who murdered Albert anyway, eh? Wouldn't that be something? All right, sir. Let me tell you about the other kind of fake, and then we shall drink some more fine German beer, eh?"

I smiled. "That sounds fine."

"Stamps can be doctored. Altered, sir, in small ways that can enhance their value. Perforations can be changed, for example. That creates an entirely different stamp. Or they can be cut off to create imperforates. Or added to previously unperforated stamps. Overprints can be added. Stamps can be regummed. All of these things make a different stamp from the original, sir. The average man cannot detect such doctoring.

That is why a collector should make his purchases only from a reputable dealer."

"Could a person create a forgery – or a fake – of the Dutch Blue Error?"

Graustein cocked his head in amusement at me. "To attempt such a thing, sir, would be a monumental waste of time. Monumental."

I nodded. That had been Ollie Weston's opinion, I recalled. In fact, aside from some myths about the Blue Error that Ollie had neglected to tell me, Morris Graustein had convinced me that Ollie hadn't lied about the stamp.

"Mr. Graustein . . ."

"Morris. Call me Morris, my friend."

"Morris," I said, "you've been a big help to me. I do appreciate it."

"Oh, it has been my pleasure, sir." He raised his glass to me and dipped his head. "My pleasure," he repeated.

I noticed that his glass was nearly empty. "I suppose we really ought to have one more," I said.

"Yes, sir. I think we ought. One more glass of this magnificent German beer is what we ought to have."

Chapter 12

When I was in College I could tuck away a couple of six-packs in an evening, no sweat. If I respected the demands of my bladder, I could drink beer all day and all night.

No more. My bladder continues to cry for attention, but in addition my eyes grow heavy, my stomach churns and gurgles, my intestines begin to snarl and kink, and a dull meat cleaver commences a slow descent through the center of my forehead.

When Morris Graustein and I finally bumbled out of the little bar on Washington Street, night had fallen and the Combat Zone had sprung to life. Red and green neon flashes jabbed painfully at my eyes. The insistent beat of amplified music – what my son Joey had once told me was called "heavy metal" – reverberated in my liquid brain. Graustein shook my hand vigorously, thanked me for the fine beer, and disappeared among the crowds on the street.

I had no interest in the business establishments, nor did the ladies moving in and out of them arouse my curiosity. I wanted only to go home and vomit.

The subway ride did nothing to ease my misery. I stumbled into my apartment, put the heat on under the water, and climbed into the shower, leaving a trail of clothing behind me. I adjusted the flow for faster and hotter than I could normally stand it. Steam filled the room. I breathed the humid air deeply. I thought that if I quit smoking cigarettes I might be able to drink better. I thought that if I quit drinking I could smoke better. I thought that if I quit doing both I could live longer.

I thought none of that would be any fun.

I dialed Deborah's home number. It rang three times before I heard a click and then her recorded voice. "This is Deborah Martinelli," said the voice. *I'm all business,* her tone made clear. *I'm an important executive lady, not to be mistaken for a fluff-headed girl. I don't play. So don't mess around.* "I can't come to the phone right now. When you hear the tone, please leave your name and message. I'll get back to you as soon as I can." There was a pause, and then she continued, a different edge to her voice. "And if that's you again, Philip, the answer is still no, it will always be no, and you needn't leave a message. Just stop calling me, will you?"

Then I heard the beep. I cleared my throat. Talking to an answering machine inhibits me. It's like being interviewed for television, which has happened to me a couple of times. I can't think of anything intelligent to say. I mumble. My syntax goes all to hell. I grin foolishly.

Once outside a courtroom where I had just finished winning a hefty award in damages from the city of Lawrence for a client who had been run over by a school bus, a reporter touched my arm and asked if I would mind answering a few questions. Behind him stood a fat, bearded man with a camera perched on his shoulder like a parrot on a pirate. The camera was trained on me. A crowd of people quickly ringed the reporter, the cameraman, and me.

"Ready, Sal?" said the reporter. The cameraman thrust up his thumb. The reporter then turned to me. "All set, Mr. Coyne?"

I smiled stiffly and nodded.

The reporter glanced at the cameraman, hesitated, then said, "I'm here at the Lawrence courthouse with Brady Coyne, the attorney for Jacqueline Callahan, who has just been awarded three-quarters of a million dollars damages for injuries sustained in an accident with a city school bus last December. Mr. Coyne," he said, turning suddenly to me and smiling his dazzling television smile, "do you expect the city to appeal this decision?"

"Well, jeez, I dunno. I mean, hey, I suppose I would. Wouldn't you?" That was my speech – this from the same attorney who had the previous afternoon delivered without notes a fifty-minute summation, a model of grammatical exactitude and verbal dexterity. "Jeez, I dunno."

When I heard myself speak, I looked at the reporter and said, "Hey, I hope this is on tape. Let me try it again, huh?"

"This is the live 'Action Cam,' Mr. Coyne," purred the reporter. He turned to the camera. "Well, that's the word from the victorious attorney here live at the Lawrence courthouse, Frank and Jenny. Now back to you."

I felt equally daunted by Deborah's answering machine. I considered hanging up. Then I figured this was as close as it appeared I was going to get to speaking to her.

"I tried to reach you several times today," I said to her machine. "I hate talking to machines, by the way. Though your Darlene isn't a hell of a lot friendlier. And maybe she doesn't deliver messages. Anyway, to say hi, really. And to suggest you find someplace else to crash for a few days, just in case our friend should decide to pay you another visit. Maybe that's what you've done already. Maybe that's why you're not home. Oh, hell. The real reason I called originally was to see if you'd like to have dinner with me tonight. Too late for that, I guess. God, I sound inane. Look. I've been doing some thinking about the stamp, and there's a question I forgot to ask you. So call me, will you?"

I hung up, wishing there was some way I could erase my speech.

I dug out a couple of my old Stan Getz records and put them on the stereo. I realized that I wanted to see Deborah badly. I padded on bare feet into the kitchen and studied my sparse collection of canned goods. No beef stew, no canned spaghetti, no hash. I settled on a can of Friend's pork and beans. I cranked it open and put it on medium heat. Then I levered the top off the last bottle of Molson's in my refrigerator.

The phone rang.

"I'm home," said Deborah. "What about the stamp?"

"Hi."

"What about the stamp?"

"Look. It's nothing. Really. I just was concerned about you. You okay? Do you think you should be staying there tonight?"

"I'll be fine. Darlene's with me. She'll stay with me the whole night."

"Aha," I said.

"What the hell does 'aha' mean?"

"Aha. The *whole* night. I get it."

"You get *what*?"

"Come on, Deborah. I woke up. I told you, I always wake up early. You were sleeping, I was awake. So I came home to change before work, that's all. I tried to write you a note. I couldn't do justice . . ."

"I don't know what you're talking about," she said.

"Can you talk?"

"Not really. Just a minute, okay?"

I heard muffled voices. Deborah said, "Hang on, will you?" to me, and then there were more voices.

Then I heard her sigh. "Okay. We can talk."

"So about last night . . ."

"Don't worry about last night. No obligation. No problem."

"I thought, my leaving like that . . ."

"Why should I care about that?"

"I just figured, your not answering my calls . . ."

"I've been busy. I *do* work, you know. Anyhow, I did. I just called you."

"Well," I said lamely, "I assumed . . ."

"What? That I'd accuse you of seducing me? That my delicate feelings would be bruised because you snuck away before I woke up so I would be deprived of the privilege of lavishing a fancy breakfast on my conquering hero after he has swept me off my feet? Come off it, Coyne."

"Oh," I said.

"You forgetting how it happened? It was *me* who crawled into *your* bed. Remember? It was *me* who . . ."

"I *do* remember, Deborah."

"Well, okay. Did you like it?"

"Yes."

"Me, too."

"I was thinking maybe we could have dinner together," I said.

"I told you. No obligation. It's all right. We're square. Even steven."

"You don't want to have dinner with me?"

"I don't want you to feel like you have to repay me for the use of my body."

"That's not . . ."

"Yes, it is," she said firmly. "You are so damn old-fashioned. You think you should feel guilty because we – my goodness, I was going to say 'fucked,' but I wouldn't want to offend – because we knew each other in a carnal sort of way. So you keep calling me, you want to make it up to me, to appease your Victorian conscience. Hey, forget it. You owe me nothing. I liked it."

"You know," I said after a moment, "I think you're right. I felt, I guess, that I was taking advantage of you, somehow. And that leaving like I did just made it worse. You're not upset?"

"Hell, yes, I'm upset. I'm upset that you can't see me as a person, but as some character in a nineteenth-century English novel."

"I think I'm beginning to get the picture."

"Well, good."

"So. How about dinner?"

"You really don't have to do this."

"God damn it, I *want* to do this."

"I don't think dinner."

"Look . . ."

"I think a movie."

"A *movie?*"

"Yeah. A movie. Anything wrong with taking a girl to a movie? Not sophisticated enough for the big-city lawyer? Don't forget, I know you're a closet popcorn freak, so don't try to fool me. Anyhow, we'll make it an Italian movie. With subtitles. That sophisticated enough for you?"

"Sure. It probably won't compare to James Bond, but it'll probably do."

"There's a little theater in Maynard. Know it?"

"Suppose I pick you up there."

"Here? At home?"

"Sure. Make it a proper date."

"Maybe a little fooling around before we leave?"

"No, I didn't mean that. It would just . . ."

"I rather thought we'd save the fooling around for afterward," she said. "So meet me at the theater. I really want to see the film."

"Well, okay."

"Know where it is?"

"I'll find it."

"What about the stamp?"

"Oh. That." I hesitated. "Okay, I admit it. That was to try to persuade you to call me."

"You lied, then, eh? No news on the stamp?"

"I did have a question which is related. It's this. Do you know where your father kept his handgun?"

"He didn't have a gun."

"He had one when I was with him."

"I'm sure he didn't own a gun."

"Oh, well," I said.

"Why? What about a gun?"

"The police are looking for a twenty-two caliber pistol. When I met your father, he said he had a twenty-two in his pocket. Albert Dopplinger was killed with a twenty-two."

"But I thought..."

"Sure. Albert was killed after your father. It just seemed there might be a link."

"Well, of *course* there's a link," she said. "Somebody killed him, then he killed your friend Albert, then he broke into my house." Her voice went low and dramatic. "Will he bash my head in, do you think, or will he shoot me?"

"Jesus, Deborah."

"Fear not. Darlene will protect me. Believe me, she is fearsome. Speaking of which – or of whom – she's coming back in now. So I better hang up. See you."

"Maynard. About nine."

"Yes."

Deborah was waiting for me in the lobby of the theater in Maynard. She hugged a big cardboard bucket to her chest. When she saw me she held up the bucket and grinned. "Popcorn. I've got the tickets. It's about to start. Let's go in."

The film had no plot that I could discern.

The scene kept shifting from idle rich, middle-aged Italians lounging aboard a yacht moored in the deserted cove of a tropical island to black-and-white flashbacks of a World War II internment center. First we were treated to close-ups of lush flesh, all bronze and copper, strapped into bikinis. Then a sudden shift to protruding ribs, empty eyes, and fingers picking at scabs. Peeled fruits – papayas, mangoes, bananas – slipping between shiny red lips. An infant with a distended belly sucking at a flaccid breast. Beringed fingers languidly wandering over fat thighs, brushing blond hair, gripping a wet cocktail glass. Shaved skulls and toothless grimaces.

All overlaid with a heavy Wagnerian score.

Afterward we had coffee at Deborah's kitchen table.

"It was a sad film, didn't you think?" she said.

"It was a sad excuse for a film."

"Not enough action for you?"

"I just don't like having my symbols crammed down my craw, that's all. Every Italian film I've ever seen seems hell-bent on expiating the great Fascist guilt."

She shrugged. "The popcorn was good."

"The popcorn was the second-best I've had recently."

"You going to stay for breakfast this time?"

"Maybe. Maybe not."

"Up to you," she said.

I woke up in the gray dawn to the honking of migrating Canada geese. I pictured the big wedge in the sky on its southward journey. Hudson Bay to Chesapeake Bay. Rain pattered gently outside, dripping onto the roof from the pines that towered over it. A soft breeze sloughed through the branches.

Deborah lay on her back beside me, her black hair fanned out over the pillow. She breathed through her mouth. Her head was turned toward me. Her hand rested lightly on my thigh. I lifted myself onto my elbow and bent over to kiss her forehead. Her silver eyes snapped open.

"You leaving?"

"Go to sleep," I said.

"Call me sometime," she mumbled, her eyes falling shut.

"I'm staying for breakfast," I said.

The clamor of the geese had faded into the damp dawn. The rain still sifted through the pines. I lay pack into Deborah's warm bed and slept.

241

Chapter 13

Zerk and I worked late on Thursday. The paperwork had been piling up, and I wanted to clean it away before the weekend. Deborah and I were driving to the Cape on Saturday. We'd take potluck at whatever restaurants might still be open and find a room in an old country inn. We'd see how many lighthouses we could find, we'd walk the beaches with our shoes in our hands, and we'd make love several times. I didn't want to have to worry about my business.

I ran out around seven o'clock and brought back ham and Swiss cheese sandwiches and coffee while Zerk typed in the blanks on a couple of wills. While we ate, I grilled him on Massachusetts contract law. I told him I thought he was ready to take the bar exam any time. Then we went back to work.

At nine o'clock I said to him, "Let's get the hell out of here."

"We're nowhere near done," he said.

"Fill your briefcase. We'll take it to my place."

He shrugged. "Sure."

He followed me in his own car. When we got to my apartment building on Atlantic Avenue I told Jerry, the guard at the gate to the underground parking garage, that a man in a yellow Volkswagen would be right along. His name was Garrett, he was my associate, and he should be allowed to park in the visitors' section. Then I rode down the ramp, and when the bar lifted I drove in, circled around a couple of concrete pillars, and tucked my BMW into my reserved parking slot.

I grabbed my briefcase, slung my topcoat over my arm, locked up the car, and went to the elevator. Zerk would have to park on the other side of the lot, and it would take him a couple of minutes to walk across to the elevator. I poked the Up button and waited for the box to slide down the cables to me. I leaned against the cement wall, sighed deeply, and lit a Winston.

When the soft voice murmured into my ear, I felt as if a spider was crawling up the back of my neck. I had heard that voice before. Most recently it had said, "Sorry, pal," shortly before I tumbled into an unwelcome chloroform sleep. It took me a moment to remember the other time I had heard it.

243

"Just relax, Mr. Coyne," the voice said. "I'm going to be going along with you."

He had a narrow, sly face and a neatly trimmed black beard salted with gray. Both of his hands were thrust into the side pockets of his coat. One of the pockets bulged.

"Why, it's Mr. Schwartz," I said. "Haven't seen you since Shaughnessey's wake."

He smiled and inclined his head. "I'm flattered that you remember me."

"Friend of Francis Shaughnessey is a friend of mine," I said. "What can I do for you?"

"Take me to your apartment. And don't try anything, please. This is a gun in my pocket."

"This is really tacky."

His smile was decidedly hostile. "I'm sorry if my style offends you. Perhaps I lack imagination."

The bell on the elevator chimed. As the doors slid open I saw Zerk hurrying toward us.

"Get in," said Schwartz. One hand grabbed my arm to steer me. The other remained in his coat pocket.

Zerk hurried to the elevator and raised his hand. I swiveled quickly away from him and stepped in. Schwartz followed me. I turned to face the open door with Schwartz standing close beside me. I felt the gun poking into my waist. As Zerk approached the elevator the door slid shut. I looked away from him. Schwartz jabbed the button for the sixth floor. My floor.

"What do you want?" I said to him, as I felt the lift of the elevator.

"The stamp, of course."

"You?"

"Yes, Mr. Coyne. It is I who knows that your client, Oliver Hazard Perry Weston, owns the Dutch Blue Error. And I believe I am correct in deducting that you are in possession of the duplicate."

I nodded. "Clever you."

Schwartz chuckled dryly.

"Is that the same gun you used to assassinate Albert Dopplinger?" I said.

Schwartz snorted. "I fail to be amused by your circumlocutions, Mr. Coyne. Clearly you were the one who murdered the poor man. I was witness to it, as you no doubt have discerned. A piece of knowledge I am prepared to barter for the stamp."

"You needn't have broken into the girl's house," I said.

"A forlorn hope, I concur. I should have thought of you sooner." Schwartz nudged

245

me again with his gun. "This time I will make no mistake."

"Watch out, boys. I think he means business."

"You're quite witty, Mr. Coyne."

"Thank you."

The elevator lurched to a stop at the sixth floor. Schwartz and I stepped out.

"Just act natural, Mr. Coyne," he said, his voice low and conspiratorial. "We're just coming home after a long day at the office."

"I think I've seen this movie already," I said.

I turned right to walk to my apartment at the end of the corridor. Schwartz was right behind me.

It all fit together. I hoped to find the lie that Charlie McDevitt told me to look for. Someone had murdered two men for a rare stamp and had not found it. He was still looking for it. He thought I had it. Schwartz, I knew now, was that man. He would keep murdering until he found it. Deborah was next. No. He would kill me next.

My only hope was Schwartz's assumption that I had the Dutch Blue Error. Perhaps he wouldn't let me die until he had the stamp.

But Schwartz didn't have the stamp himself, and that confused me. It meant that

246

somebody else did. And that meant there was another lie I had to discover.

As Schwartz and I arrived at the door to my apartment, I saw Zerk emerge from the door of the stairwell at the far end of the corridor. He turned and walked in our direction. I took the keys from my pocket, fumbled with them at the door, then dropped them.

"No tricks," hissed Schwartz.

As I bent for the keys I glanced in Zerk's direction. His face was impassive as he walked toward us, toting his briefcase. A tired young executive after a long day at the office. He glanced casually at me and Schwartz, not a trace of recognition in his eyes. From my bent-position I darted a quick glance back over my shoulder toward Schwartz. My eyes begged Zerk not to stop, not to recognize me, not to speak. Go call a cop, my glance screamed at him. Stay away from this man with a gun.

I straightened up, the keys in my hand. Zerk continued past us. He didn't pause or even nod to us. The door to my apartment opened, and I stepped inside. Schwartz was right behind me.

When the side of Zerk's hand met the flesh at the back of Schwartz's neck, it made the same dull thud that my mother's meat mallet used to make when she pounded out veal on the board in our kitchen. Schwartz sighed and fell against me. I grabbed his arms, and pulled him into my apartment. Zerk followed, grinning broadly.

Schwartz lay limp and still on the carpet in my living room. I reached into his coat pocket and removed the little automatic. I held it up for Zerk to see.

"I know," he said. "When I saw him down there in the garage, I thought you have picked up Peter Lorre or Edward G. Robinson for a companion." He held out his hand and I gave him the gun. "Little Colt," he said. "Twenty-two." He poked at the weapon and several cartridges slid out into his hand. He held one up between his thumb and forefinger for me to see. "Hollow-point long rifle," he said. "Nasty. They make a tiny little hole going in and a great big mess inside."

"A twenty-two killed Albert Dopplinger."

Zerk raised his eyebrows. "So who the hell is this, anyway?"

I glanced down at the motionless body on the floor. "Unless I miss my guess, this is the man who murdered Francis Shaughnessey and Albert Dopplinger. The man who broke into Deborah Martinelli's house. The man

248

who wants the Dutch Blue Error duplicate stamp badly enough to kill for it."

"And," added Zerk, "the man the police want. Instead of me."

I nodded. Schwartz's head seemed to be twisted at an odd angle as he lay on the floor. "Did you kill him?" I asked Zerk.

"No. Could have. Figured whoever he was and whatever his business was with you, we could do that later if we wanted to."

I frowned at him, and he held up his hand. "Just kidding. He should be coming around in a minute. He's okay. Just a tap."

"It didn't sound like a tap."

"Relatively speaking."

As if he had been listening, Schwartz groaned and opened his eyes. He blinked a couple of times. His forehead wrinkled with effort as he moved his head. His hand went to the back of his neck. "Oh, Jesus," he said.

"Good morning, Mr. Schwartz," I said pleasantly. "Toast and juice? Buttered bun? Eggs?"

He frowned at me. "Ah. Mr. Coyne."

I bowed. "At your service." I inclined my head toward Zerk. "My colleague, Mr. Garrett."

Schwartz's eyes darted to Zerk, who obliged him with a broad, white-toothed grin. "Yassah, boss," he drawled.

Schwartz pushed himself gingerly up against the wall into a sitting position. He rubbed the back of his neck and smiled ruefully at me. "So you've got the drop on me, Mr. Coyne. No matter. We shall transact some business."

"Really?"

"Oh, surely, Mr. Coyne. That's why I came here. You need me. I will help you to dispose of this valuable scrap of paper that you possess. I have certain contacts. I have information that you need. Pertaining to your client, Mr. Weston. Together, you and I, we shall reap great rewards." He attempted to smile. It appeared to pain him.

"I don't have the stamp," I said. "And I don't think you know anything that I don't know. And," I added, "somehow I don't think you came here to bargain with me."

"Ah, Mr. Coyne," he said, shaking his head sadly. "I can help you. You will see. You don't need to lie to me. Of course you have the stamp. So let us confer."

"You came here with a gun to confer, did you?"

He shrugged. "I needed your attention."

"Well, I don't bargain with murderers," I said. "Against my professional ethics, you know." I turned to Zerk. "You want the pleasure of calling Leo Kirk?"

Zerk's mouth tightened. "No."

I went to the kitchen wall and reached for the telephone. Schwartz's eyebrows shot up. "What are you doing?"

"Calling the police, of course."

"Okay. You win. You're not bluffing, Mr. Coyne. I'll tell you."

"You've got nothing to tell me that you can't tell the police."

"This is ridiculous," pleaded Schwartz. He tried to stand up, then sank back into a sitting position against the wall. "I didn't kill anyone," he muttered.

I dialed Kirk's precinct station.

"How do you think I know that Weston owns the original Dutch Blue Error?" said Schwartz.

I shrugged and smiled. "Lieutenant Kirk, please," I said into the telephone.

"Is he bluffing me?" Schwartz said to Zerk. Zerk replied with an exaggerated shrug of his thick shoulders and widened eyes. "Hang up," said Schwartz. "I didn't do anything. Let me tell you about Guillaume Lundi."

Kirk came onto the line. I told him to come on over and pick up Francis Shaughnessey's killer. I asked him to leave his partner, Stone, there. He said he would do both. Then I hung up.

Schwartz had slumped back down so that only his head was propped against the wall, with the rest of his body stretched out on the floor. His eyes were closed. His skin had an unhealthy grayish tinge beneath a sheen of perspiration. His breathing came harshly through his open mouth.

"What about this Lundi?" I said to him.

"Don't feel too good," he whispered between clenched teeth.

"Concussion, probably," observed Zerk. "He'll probably puke in a minute."

"Oh, Christ. On my rug."

Leo Kirk arrived, a pair of burly uniformed policemen in tow, within half an hour of my call. By the time Schwartz had deposited his supper into the shopping bag I held for him, splashed water onto his face under Zerk's careful supervision, and proclaimed himself much improved.

Kirk read him his rights and informed him he was being placed under arrest for suspicion of murder, assault, carrying a concealed weapon, and a few other things that he rattled off too quickly for me to catch, and then sent him off with the two policemen. Then he and Zerk and I sat at my kitchen table.

"Here's the gun," I said, handing the Colt automatic to Kirk. "It's a twenty-two."

252

"Yes, I can see that," he said dryly. He tucked it into his jacket pocket. "I'll get it over to Mullins in Cambridge for ballistics. Since both of you guys have fondled it, no sense in looking for prints, I guess."

"Sorry about that," I said. "He didn't hand it to us willingly, you know."

"Doesn't matter. You got beer or something?" When I raised my eyebrows, he added, "Went off duty an hour ago. I was halfway out the door when your call came."

I dug two cans of Budweiser and one Schlitz out of my refrigerator.

"Chips? Pretzels?" Kirk grinned.

"Nope."

He sighed and tilted the can of Bud to his mouth. His throat worked at it for a moment, and then he thumped the can down on the table, grunted "Ahh!", and wiped his mouth with the back of his hand. "Now. Tell me what you make of this."

"I'm just guessing," I said.

"So guess, then."

"Okay. Here goes. Shaughnessey's in Europe. He worked there for years. He's got contacts. He's a collector. Somebody puts him onto this stamp. It's the duplicate of one that the philatelic world assumed was one-of-a-kind. Very valuable. Priceless. His source is probably not entirely legitimate, so he gets it for a good price. He's convinced it's legitimate. Probably has it looked at by somebody who can verify that sort of thing. He brings it back and begins to ask around. Very discreetly. He finally makes contact with this Schwartz, who somehow knows that Ollie Weston owns the original Blue Error. Schwartz and Shaughnessey meet. My guess is that Schwartz insisted on a face-to-face meeting. Perhaps he also insisted on seeing the stamp. In any case, he verified that the stamp Shaughnessey had was genuine – and therefore enormously valuable. They probably met in a public place, so Schwartz couldn't make a move for the stamp then. He found out where Shaughnessey lived and broke in through the glass door by the garden. Possibly he intended to ransack the place while Shaughnessey was gone, and he came home unexpectedly. Maybe he went there when Shaughnessey was home on purpose, in order to coerce the whereabouts of the stamp from him. Maybe he even went with an offer to buy the stamp. Whatever. It didn't work out, and Schwartz ended up smashing in Shaughnessey's skull."

"But he didn't get the stamp," said Kirk.

"No. Either Shaughnessey refused to tell him where it was hidden, or else he came home while Schwartz was tearing the place apart and Schwartz hit him from behind. In either case, Schwartz's next stop was Albert Dopplinger. Maybe, in order to get rid of him, Shaughnessey told Schwartz that Dopplinger actually had it. Or maybe Schwartz went to him for information. In any case, he made an appointment to see Albert at the museum. Dopplinger must've been suspicious, or had second thoughts, because he called me. I figure I got there very soon after Schwartz shot Albert in the head."

"Why did he shoot Dopplinger?" interrupted Kirk. "How do you figure that?"

I shrugged. "He concluded that Albert didn't have the stamp, and didn't know who did have it. By then Schwartz had gone too far. Albert would have figured out that Schwartz had killed Shaughnessey. Having killed once, the second time was easy. I don't know. In any case, when I got there, Schwartz was still in the room. He heard me at the door, so he turned off the lights and hid behind one of the cabinets or counters. I entered the room, turned on the lights, and saw Albert. When I knelt beside the body, Schwartz came up behind me and chloroformed me. At that point he probably heard Zerk coming along and hid himself again, and slipped out after Zerk had taken me away."

Zerk nodded. "He could've still been there. I didn't look around."

"If you hadn't come, he might've shot me, too," I said.

Kirk nodded impatiently. "Then what?"

"So he didn't find the stamp. His next stop was Deborah Martinelli's house in Carlisle. Shaughnessey's daughter. He broke in there last weekend. He didn't find it there, either. Because it's not there. So Schwartz figured it might be me who had the stamp. Or at least knew where it was. That's why he came here tonight."

I shrugged and looked at Kirk. "Make sense?"

"Very neat," he said.

"You don't buy it?"

"No, no," he said distractedly, waving his hand, "it makes sense." Then he turned to me. "Couple of things do bother me though."

"Like what?"

"Well, the two murders, for one thing. Very different. In one case we have a skull smashed in with the base of a statue. Messy. Amateur night. In the second, we have a neat assassination with a small-caliber pistol. And the victim was chloroformed first. Premeditated, professional, tidy. Okay? One messy murder, evidently provoked by anger

256

of frustration or desperation. And one clean, businesslike kill. That bothers me. That doesn't seem like the work of the same man."

"So he killed Shaughnessey," said Zerk, "and then figured, what the hell, next time I'll do it right."

Kirk nodded. "Maybe." He paused. "But then why does he go to the lady's house when she's not home? Why not go after her like he did Dopplinger?"

Neither Zerk nor I answered him.

"The other thing that bothers me," continued Kirk, "is this. Where's the stamp?"

"Good question," I said. "But it really doesn't change anything."

"The lady could have the stamp," he persisted. "Say she's had it all the time. She wouldn't leave it lying around for some casual prowler to find. She'd have it hidden away. Everything would make sense if she had it."

"You saying she killed her own father? And Albert, too?"

"I'm not saying anything," said Kirk, holding the beer can against his cheek and closing his eyes. "Just speculating. It's what we cops do. Speculate."

"What would she have to gain by keeping the stamp? Why wouldn't she just sell it?"

Kirk opened his eyes. "I dunno. Nothing, I guess. At least, not if she didn't kill anybody."

"More likely Shaughnessey hid it where it'll never be found," I said.

Kirk shrugged. "You're probably right. We'll know more when we check up on Schwartz and get a ballistics report on his little gun." He drained his beer and abruptly stood up. "I best be getting back. I'm eager to interrogate Mr. Schwartz."

"I thought you were off duty."

"A good cop," he replied, thrusting back his shoulders, "is never off duty."

"My hero," I said.

Kirk paused at the door, then turned to Zerk. "Mr. Garrett, this makes things a lot better for you, you know."

Zerk scowled.

Kirk shrugged. "I'll be in touch," he said to me.

After Kirk left, I took down my bottle of Jack Daniel's and poured Zerk and me a couple of fingers, neat, into tumblers. I held my glass aloft. "To your exoneration," I said.

Zerk shook his head. "I don't know about that." But he took a sip. "That Kirk didn't seem too convinced."

"Kirk is a good cop," I said. "His job is

to be dubious. It's logical, though, isn't it? You'll see. Schwartz is our man."

Zerk emptied his glass in a gulp. "I hope you're right," he said.

"And by the way. Thanks for saving my life again." I poured more sour mash into his glass and replenished my own. "That's twice."

Zerk nodded absently. "I'll feel better when we find the damn stamp."

"We are done looking for the damn stamp," I said. "Bad fortune follows it around. This case is closed."

"Yeah. Good." I could tell by Zerk's tone that his heart wasn't in it.

Chapter 14

"Every summer Cape Cod sinks several feet into the ocean from the weight of the humanity that descends upon it," I said to Deborah as we crossed the Sagamore Bridge which spans the Cape Cod Canal. "Then, the day after Labor Day, it bubbles up again, whooshing its breath out like a man who's been under water too long, looks around, and decides it's okay again."

Deborah stared out the window on her side of the car. This October Saturday had dawned gray and cold, and Deborah's mood matched the weather. We had been driving for more than an hour from her house in Carlisle down Route 128 and then the length of Route 3 in silence. She had fiddled with the radio, finally settling on an FM station that gave us Bach and Stravinsky, and then she huddled against the car door. She hugged herself into her blue hooded sweatshirt and deflected my conversational thrusts with monosyllabic parries.

I took the first exit after the bridge onto 6A, which took us back under the bridge and would meander along the bay side of the Cape all the way to Provincetown. I like 6A. There's not a single McDonald's or Burger King its entire length. Just old Cape-style houses and lots of little shops and here and there glimpses of the ocean across salt marshes.

"Gloria and I brought the boys to the Cape for a week one summer when they were little," I said to Deborah. "We left the house in Wellesley at something like six-thirty in the morning and finally crossed the bridge at one-fifteen in the afternoon. The traffic heading south on Route 3 was stopped dead from Marshfield all the way to the canal. The boys finally got out of the car and started walking. I believe they would've got to the rotary before we did, but they stopped to talk with some people from Connecticut, who gave them Coke and potato chips. Right then I swore I'd never go to the Cape in the summer again."

"Did you?" said Deborah.

"Nope," I replied, encouraged by even that unforced conversational nudge. "That was the difference between Gloria and me. Or one of them. Gloria would wait in line forever, if it was something she wanted. Six hours in bumper-to-bumper traffic was nothing to her. And an hour in a line at a restaurant was fine. We went to Disney World once and spent more time standing in lines than doing anything else. She had a wonderful time."

"You miss her, don't you?" she said suddenly, turning in the seat to look at me. I glanced at her. She sat sideways, one leg tucked under her. Her gray eyes were solemn. Her black hair was tied back with a red kerchief. I reached over to touch her face.

"I don't think about it much," I said.

"You think about it all the time."

"I do miss the boys, if that's what you mean."

"You miss Gloria."

I shrugged. "Does that bother you?"

She turned back to peer out of the side window. "Not for the reason you think."

In Sandwich, we stopped at a little nondescript restaurant for lunch. A hand-lettered sign on the door said CLOSED FOR THE SEASON AFTER COLUMBUS DAY. Less than a week away. This was not, evidently, a place the natives patronized. We were the only customers. The walls were festooned with fishing nets and lobster buoys. Our waitress took our orders glumly, then returned to the paperback novel she was reading at a corner table. The clam chowder, we decided, had come from a can.

We drove through Barnstable, Cummaquid, Yarmouth, Dennis, and Brewster, stopping at every antique shop and art gallery we found open. In the middle of the afternoon the rain came hard and cold, angled by the east wind. The snick of the windshield wipers kept a syncopated rhythm with the cello and clarinet music from the radio.

In Eastham, Deborah suddenly sat forward. "Stop here, please," she said.

"Here?"

The sign outside the little Cape Cod-style shop read SANTA'S ELVES: CANDLES AND CHRISTMAS.

"This is nothing but a damn tourist trap," I said. But I pulled into the crushed-stone parking area. Half a dozen cars were there, wearing license plates from New York and Vermont and New Jersey.

"You don't have to come in if you don't want to," she said, and before I could reply she was out of the car and on her way into the shop.

"I won't, then," I muttered. I lit a Winston and watched the rain that sheeted on the windshield distort the stunted pines that waltzed in the wind. Across the street

I saw a little square building, hardly bigger than a fisherman's shack. A sign over the door read WALTER THISTLE, ARTIST. OPEN.

I decided I'd like to meet someone named Walter Thistle, so I dashed across the street and into Mr. Thistle's studio. A large, ginger dog thumped his tail on the floor. A wood stove simmered in a corner. A voice from another room called, "Look around. Be with you in a minute. Don't mind Gregory. He's not as fierce as he looks."

Gregory, as if to vindicate his master, rolled onto his back and began to wave all four legs in the air. I scratched his belly, which set his tail thumping at an increased tempo.

Thistle painted watercolors. Some sat on easels, some hung on the plain pine walls, and some were stacked carelessly against table legs and chairs. Thistle painted with a big brush on wet paper, a stroke here and a blob of color there miraculously creating clouds, fog, surf, sand, rocks, flowers, ships, trees.

I had imagined Walter Thistle in a long, white beard wearing a tattered flannel shirt, his baddy corduroys supported by wide red suspenders. In fact, his beard was sun-bleached blond, his body trim and athletic. His faded blue eyes and the cross-hatching of wrinkles on his cheeks merely suggested his age. I guessed he was sixty. He emerged from a doorway tucking a white dress shirt into his blue jeans.

"See anything you like?"

"I like everything," I answered. "You've got a nice style. Loose. Generous with color."

He grinned. "They accuse me of being derivative," he said. "I've shown my stuff in New York. The so-called critics laugh at it. 'Cape Cod art,' they call it. Well, hey, they're right, in a way. What they don't understand is that this Cape Cod art started with Walter Thistle. I came here in forty-six with a little chunk of shrapnel in my leg. Bought me some colors and paper and been at it ever since. Doing Cape Cod art. Been at it longer than the rest of 'em. I came here to paint, not to sell. The others, they come to the Cape in the summer to make a buck off the tourists. They see the kind of work that Walter Thistle does, they think, 'Hell, this is simple,' and they knock off some surf on the rocks, maybe a lighthouse and a beached dory, and, by God, they're right, you know? Tourists think, 'Dad gum, we've got us an authentic Cape Cod watercolor, Myrtle.' They come in here, take a look around, and they think they're seeing the

265

same old stuff. By the time they get to Eastham, see, they've already stopped in the other places. They see imitations first, they think they're the real thing. So by the time they get here, and see the real thing, they think I'm the imitator."

I bent to examine a small framed study of a sand dune and beach grass. "How much for this one?"

"Hundred fifty," he said. "There's a little sticker on the back. You can get something similar back up the road for sixty," he added. "Most folks can't tell the difference."

He sat on a straight-backed wooden chair and poked Gregory's belly with the toe of his sneaker and cocked his head at me. It struck me as a challenge.

"I don't pretend to know that much about art . . ."

"Most folks don't," he said. "You're probably best off back up the road. Tell your friends you got yourself a genuine Thistle watercolor, they'll say, 'Hey, ain't that nice, now,' and it won't be worth a damn. Cape Cod art. Humph!"

"I like it better than anything I've seen."

Thistle began to stuff tobacco into the bowl of a blackened old pipe with a curved stem. "Buy it, don't buy it. Can't promise

266

you nothing 'cept it'll get prettier and prettier the longer you look at it."

I lit a Winston and cocked an eye at him. "Hundred fifty, eh?"

Thistle sucked on his pipe. "You're probably better off back up the road."

I bought the painting, of course. I couldn't decide whether it was the beauty of the work or the perverse sales pitch of Walter Thistle that persuaded me. But I decided that I couldn't take any chance of an imitation up the road.

Thistle wrapped the painting in a big square of oilcloth and put it into a plastic shopping bag for me. I shook his hand, scratched Gregory's belly, and jogged across the street through the rain to my car. I put the painting into the trunk and I returned to my seat behind the wheel. Deborah had not returned yet.

A random thought fluttered in my brain like a butterfly, and I tried to pin down its wings so that I could examine it. Paintings and stamps. Authentic and derivative. Beauty and value. Experts and tourists. A concept flitted there, but it succeeded in evading the wild sweeps of my deductive net.

Deborah suddenly opened the door and slid into the car, shaking the rain from her hair, and, for the first time all day, smiling. She held a big paper bag in her lap.

"What'd you get?" I said.

"Nice stuff. Bayberry-scented candles. Some gifts. And look."

She reached into the bag and pulled out a little box. She opened it and handed me a tiny replica of a lobster pot, no bigger than a match box. I held it up in front of my face by the little string attached to it. Deborah leaned toward me, bracing herself with a hand on my knee.

"See," she said, her face close to mine, "it opens and closes, like this. It's even got the little netting inside. It's a Christmas tree ornament. I'll hang it on my tree to remind me of our weekend."

I held the little object in the palm of my hand and turned it over with my finger. A tiny oval label was stuck on the bottom. I read it to Deborah.

"Made in Taiwan," I said. I handed it back to her.

She grabbed it and dropped it into her paper bag. "You can be a real bastard," she said quietly, and she turned her face to the window beside her.

We rented a room in an old Victorian rooming house in Wellfleet, changed our clothes, and had roast beef at a restaurant perched on a hillside overlooking the bay. We sat by a window. The wind had blown the rain away, and we could see the clouds skidding across the face of the low-hanging harvest moon. I reached across the table to touch Deborah's hand.

"Hey," I said.

She looked up at me. "I'm sorry. I haven't been very good company."

"Me neither, I guess."

She smiled, that quick, sad smile that seemed to reserve the prerogative of transforming itself into a frown at the least provocation, and squeezed my hand.

"I have a surprise for you," I said. "I wanted to present it to you with lots of pomp and ceremony."

She smiled again. "I'm afraid I'm deflating your pomp and raining on your ceremony. I'm sorry. What's your surprise?"

"It's about your father. I think we found the man who did it."

"Who killed him, you mean."

"Yes."

She nodded. "Good."

"He's also the man who killed Albert Dopplinger, the museum man, and the same one who broke into your house. So it looks like you won't have to worry any more." I paused. "He pulled a gun on me the other night. He's the guy who chloroformed me."

"He's been busy," she said. "I'm glad they found him."

"But we still haven't found the stamp."

She shrugged and turned her face to look out the window.

"I thought you'd be happy."

"I am," she said. "That's great."

She took her hand from mine to pick up her coffee cup. I lit a cigarette.

"Look," I said. "What's the matter, anyway?"

"Nothing. Really." As if to prove her point, she turned to smile at me. Then she turned back to the window.

"If it's about that little lobster pot thing . . ."

She shook her head.

"Well, then . . ."

"Just let it be," she said, with sudden vehemence. "Okay? Let it be, huh?"

"Well, Jesus . . ."

"It's me. That's all. Leave me alone."

"I thought you'd be happy."

"I am. I'm happy."

"You show it funny."

"You don't know much about women, do you?"

I sat on the edge of the big four-poster dressed in pajamas I had bought for the occasion. I held a glass of brandy in each hand. On Deborah's pillow I had placed the Walter Thistle watercolor, still wrapped in its oilcloth.

She came out of the bathroom wrapped in her old red terrycloth robe. She sat on the bed beside me. I handed her one of the glasses.

"Cheers, then," she said, none too cheerfully.

I touched her glass with mine. "Here's to our weekend."

"One more day," she said, sipping from her glass.

"You make it sound like a prison term."

"Don't be so damned sensitive."

I reached across the bed and picked up the painting. I handed it to her.

"What's this?"

"For you," I said.

She held the package on her lap and unfolded the oilcloth. She stared down at the picture.

"It's a genuine Walter Thistle," I told her. She looked up at me, wrinkling her nose and frowning. "Never heard of Walter Thistle, eh?" I continued with a smile. "He's the genuine thing. The original Cape Cod watercolorist. All the others imitate him. But he's the one that gets accused of being the imitator. Do you like it?"

"Very much," she said softly. "Very much."

"I wasn't sure. Your father's taste in art..."

She touched my mouth with two fingers. "Shh," she said. She propped the painting on the table beside the bed, sipped her brandy, then placed her glass beside the picture. She took my glass from my hand and set it beside hers. Then she turned to face me. She frowned under her tousled hair. Her eyes stared solemnly into mine. Moving in a rhythm to music only she could hear, her hands moved down to the sash of her robe. She tugged it, and her gown fell open. She rolled her shoulders and rotated her hips in a slow-motion dance that slid the robe off her body into a puddle around her feet. Under the robe she wore a sheer, floor-length gown. It was cut square across the tops of her breasts, and hung full, touching only her bosom and hips. Its ice-blue color mirrored her eyes perfectly.

I reached out to her, but she stepped back out of my reach.

"Want me to hold you a little?" I said.

"No," she said. "No. I want you to make love to me."

Her passion seemed built from despair, her urgency from desperation, and her release, when it finally came, seemed only to lift her to a different plateau, more distant from me than before. And afterward, when she held me to her, I could feel her cheeks wet against my face.

We crept under the covers and I went to sleep with the scent of her hair in my face and her leg hooked over mine. I awoke in the blue light that came before the dawn. Deborah was sitting beside me. She hugged her legs tight to her chest, and she rested her cheek on top of her knees, facing away from me. I touched her shoulder and whispered, "Hey?"

She shrugged my hand away, and I heard her sniff.

"What is it?"

She turned to face me. Her eyes were swollen.

"It's too complicated," she said.

"Try me."

She shook her head and looked away again. "I'm still married, you know," she said.

"You're separated."

"Please don't," she said softly. "Just don't say anything."

Chapter 15

"He's an ingrate and a twerp and I don't want him to have my money!"

Dr. Douglas Segrue ran his forefinger across his prim little gray mustache and peered at me through his wire-rimmed spectacles. Fathers, I thought, seemed fated to disapprove of their sons sooner or later. I thought of Billy and Joey and wondered what was in store for me. Ollie Weston's assessment of his son, Perry, rang in my ears. "He's neither particularly bright nor particularly brave," he had said.

Fathers and daughters seemed to have it better. I was reminded of the businesslike handshake Deborah Martinelli had granted me the previous day when I dropped her off after our Cape Cod weekend. Deborah and Francis Shaughnessey did not seem to have had father-son type issues between them.

"I want you to give it some more thought, Doug," I said to my client.

He leaned his elbows on my desk. "It's my money, Brady. I can do whatever I want with it. If I wish to disown my son, I will. And you are my lawyer, and you can do it for me."

"In the first place," I said patiently, "Dave isn't a twerp. He's thirty-seven years old, he's a splendid doctor, and if he wants to devote his career to a clinic in Panama, that seems to me a fine thing. And he's not an ingrate. He's very proud of you."

"If he were proud of me, and if he weren't a twerp, he'd be taking over my practice," muttered Segrue, "instead of wasting his time with jungle savages."

"Panama City isn't a jungle. Anyway, the courts . . ."

"This is all legal. I'm of sound mind."

I cocked an eyebrow at him.

"God damn it, Brady, I *am* of sound mind." He ran the palm of his hand across the board-flat top of his crew cut. "Are you saying I'm not of sound mind?"

"I'm saying this is dumb, and it raises the logical question. Look. If Beth were alive, do you think she'd approve?"

He shrugged away the memory of his wife. "David was the plum of Beth's eye. David could do no wrong."

I glanced at my watch. Dr. Segrue had already overstayed his appointment. He caught my look and pushed himself away from my desk. "Okay," he said. "I'll think about it some more. I'm not going to die tonight. But I know what I want. There are plenty of lawyers in this town, you know."

I stood up and walked around the desk. I touched his elbow. "Plenty of good ones, too, Doug. They'll do just what you ask them. Never question your impeccable judgment. For example, they would have settled that malpractice suit out of court, just like you wanted, and it would've only cost you a hundred grand."

"Yeah, well you were right about that one," he said. "This is different."

I steered him toward the door. "Make an appointment with Mr. Garrett to see me next week, Doug. If you're still thinking this way, we'll put some things on paper. Fair enough?"

"Okay," he mumbled.

"Just do me a favor."

"What?"

"Talk to Dave."

"What do you want me to say to him?"

"Ask him if he cares what you do with your money."

Segrue blinked at me for a minute, then grinned. I'll wager the little twerp could care less."

I smiled and opened the door for him. "I'll

wager he'll have some interesting ideas on the disposition of your estate," I said.

We shook hands, and Segrue left, muttering, "Jungle clinic! Damn little twerp."

In my outer office Zerk was pounding furiously on the typewriter. Seated on the sofa across from him, magazines opened on their laps, were detectives Kirk and Stone. Their heads swiveled in unison to follow Doug Segrue out of the door, then rotated back to look at me.

"Gentlemen," I said.

They both stood up. "Got a minute?" said Kirk.

I jerked my head toward my office. "Come on in."

The tempo of Zerk's typing seemed to increase as the two detectives followed me in. We sat around the coffee table in the corner of my office.

"Did Zerk offer you coffee?"

"He didn't offer us the time of day," growled Stone. "Told us you were busy."

"I was," I said. "Want some?"

Leo Kirk shook his head. "Thought you'd like to know. Mr. Schwartz isn't our man."

"Oh?"

"He was in New York the night Francis

Shaughnessey was killed. His gun is not the one that shot Albert Dopplinger."

I raised my eyebrows. "But he was there. He admitted that. He chloroformed me."

"He admits he was there, yes. Says Dopplinger called him."

"Just like he supposedly called you," added Stone.

"Matter of fact," continued Kirk, "he said he saw you standing over his body."

"You knew that," I said. "Listen. What are you implying?"

"It's pretty obvious," said Stone.

"Nothing," said Kirk quickly. "I'm not implying anything. Just that this Schwartz seems as clean as you, and we're back to square one on this thing. The Dopplinger case belongs to Cambridge, anyway. And we're certain Schwartz had nothing to do with the Shaughnessey thing – which *is* our problem."

"And that boy out there," said Stone, "ain't off the hook."

"Now, listen..."

"Relax," said Kirk. "I just wanted you to know, since you are, er, involved in this."

I thought for a minute. "What about his pulling a gun on me? Doesn't that signify something?"

"Did he *pull* a gun on you?"

"He had it in his pocket. He forced me into the elevator."

"Did you see the gun?"

"Well, sure."

"I mean before your friend hit him."

"I saw it in his pocket."

"He wanted to prosecute your friend," said Stone. "For assault."

"Oh, Jesus," I said. "That's ridiculous."

"We talked him out of it," said Kirk.

"*You* talked him out of it," said Stone.

"This guy," I said, "chloroformed me. He broke into Deborah Martinelli's house. Are you saying you're letting him off scot-free?"

"Look, Mr. Coyne," said Kirk. "Schwartz admitted none of that to us. He said he went to Dopplinger's lab when he was invited, peeked in the open door, saw you standing over the body, turned around and left. Matter of fact, he was the one who called it in. Apologized profusely for not leaving his name or sticking around. He said he was walking to your apartment with you when he was struck from behind. He had a weapon in his pocket, he admitted. He has a license. He deals in valuable objects. As for Mrs. Martinelli's house, that is matter for the Carlisle police. I have communicated with them. They didn't seem particularly inclined to pursue it, inasmuch as nothing was stolen and nobody was harmed."

"And he was in New York when Shaughnessey was murdered."

"Yes."

"But he came to the funeral."

Kirk nodded. "Sure I saw him there myself. He said Shaughnessey had been a client of his. Schwartz deals in art objects. Buys in Europe, mostly, sells in the United States. Has offices in New York and Boston. He's well placed in the business of importing valuable collectibles."

"So what the hell did he want from me?" I said.

Kirk shrugged. "I'm not sure. He said he knew you were interested in that stamp. Said he felt that the two of you might put your heads together. That's how he put it. He seemed surprised that you claimed to feel threatened."

"He was poking me with the goddam gun," I said.

"According to him, he asked if you could talk, you shrugged and said you were tired, and he went up the elevator with you and you didn't tell him not to. Then Mr. Garrett snuck up on him and cold-cocked him."

"That," I said, more loudly than was necessary, "is *not* the way it happened."

Kirk sighed. "You want to press charges?"

I looked at the two detectives. Stone was grinning at me. "No," I said. "I guess not. Tell Schwartz I would like to talk to him, though, would you?"

"Can't do that," said Kirk.

"Why not?"

"Schwartz went back to New York."

"You're lucky he's not pressing charges against your boy out there," added Stone.

They stood up. I took Kirk's hand. Stone didn't offer his, nor did I to him. "Sorry this didn't pan out," said Kirk.

"He's lying, you know," I said.

Kirk nodded. "He's lying about some of it, I'm sure. But he didn't murder Shaughnessey, and his gun didn't kill Dopplinger, and we've got nothing on him. But don't be discouraged. Something'll turn up."

"We've already got a good suspect," said Stone, his fat jowls puffed in a smile.

"Zerk didn't do anything, and you know it."

When they left, Zerk stopped typing and swiveled in his chair to glower at me. I summarized what they had told me. The creases of his frown deepened as he heard the story. When I finished, he said, "Yeah. That figures."

281

"Well," I said, "he *didn't* murder anybody."

"He could've shot Dopplinger with a different gun."

"So could you or I. Or anyone else."

Zerk snorted and turned his back on me. His typewriter resumed its rapid-fire clacking. I shrugged and returned to my office.

It was several hours later that same Monday afternoon when Zerk buzzed me.

I picked up my phone. "What is it?"

"Phone call. Long distance. Guess who?"

"I'm not in the mood for games, Zerk. Who is it?"

"Our friend. Schwartz."

"Well, okay," I said slowly. "Why don't you listen in?"

"Will do."

I heard a click. "Mr. Schwartz," I said.

"Mr. Coyne," he said. "We have some unfinished business."

"We do?"

"We do. The gendarmes have released me from their clutches. An unfortunate misunderstanding. But I bear you no grudge." He paused. "Now, then. I have concluded that you do not possess the duplicate Dutch Blue Error, nor does Mrs.

Martinelli, and you don't know where it is. Am I correct?"

"Yes."

"Then my apologies for my discourtesy last Thursday."

"Okay."

"And I accept any apologies you might care to extend with regard to your friend's treatment of me."

I said nothing.

"I apologize also for the unfortunate necessity of rendering you comatose in Mr. Dopplinger's laboratory, as well. Naturally, I assumed you had murdered the poor man. When I subsequently found no weapon, I admit I was puzzled. I did, in any case, require the opportunity to search your person as well as Mr. Dopplinger's."

"For the stamp."

"For the stamp, yes. And, failing that, for Mr. Dopplinger's notebook. Neither of which I found, of course."

"So you called to apologize. Well, thanks."

I heard him chuckle. "I didn't call to apologize. That was gratuitous. I called to share some information with you. Information that could enable you to find the stamp."

"And if I do, I might do business with you," I said.

"Ah, Mr. Coyne. You do not disappoint me."

"If I find the stamp, I sell it to you. Is that it?"

"Let us say, you'll allow me the opportunity to make the first offer."

"If I find the stamp, Mr. Schwartz, it won't be mine to offer for sale."

"Ah, quite so. That, of course, is entirely up to you. It belongs, as patrimony, to Mrs. Martinelli. Perhaps you would suggest to her how she might profitably dispose of the item, then."

I thought for a minute. "I suppose," I said slowly, "that could be done. Provided I find the stamp."

"Consider what I tell you," said Schwartz. I heard him sigh deeply. "My, ah, interest in the so-called Dutch Blue Error goes back well before the events in Paris and San Juan in 1967 of which I am about to speak. My involvement has not been altogether, shall we say, ethical. I have not, on the other hand, participated in homicide, which is considerably more than can be said for the other players in the drama of the Blue Error. I want you to understand that. I have killed no one, nor have I abetted anyone who has. Nevertheless, several men have died. The

284

first was an innocent Parisian purchasing agent named Guillaume Lundi..."

As Schwartz talked I jotted notes onto a yellow legal pad. He talked for fifteen minutes or so in that precise diction of his. My mind swirled with possibilities. I underlined several words on my notepad, drew arrows from this point to that, punctuated some of Schwartz's bits of information with question marks and exclamation points.

"So that," he said finally, "is how Francis Shaughnessey and I came to know each other. My role in the entire matter had not been completely honorable, of course. On the other hand, I have given value for value. As things presently stand, my unique knowledge that your Mr. Weston possesses the original stamp has lost its marketability. Hence I come to you."

"I'll have to give it some thought," I said cautiously.

I heard Schwartz chuckle. "A devilish puzzle, I grant you. I trust I have helped you to sort out some of the pieces."

"Perhaps."

"Good day, then, Mr. Coyne. Please call me should there be some business for us to transact."

He gave me his phone number in New

York and hung up. After I heard the click I said into the phone, "You still there?"

"Yup," said Zerk.

"What'd you think?"

"Wow!"

"Yeah. That's what I thought, too. Look. Hold any calls. I've got some thinking to do."

I replaced the telephone and studied the several pages of notes I had taken. Charlie McDevitt had advised me to presume some lies. Suddenly I had more candidates than I knew what to do with.

I sucked on Winstons, outlined scenarios, and after an hour I dropped my pencil onto my desk, pushed myself back, and whispered, "Of course!"

I rang Ollie Weston's number. Perry answered.

"It's Brady Coyne," I said.

"Oh. Hi."

"I'd like to see your father this evening," I said. "Any problem with that?"

"He doesn't go anywhere."

"Good. And Perry?"

"Yes?"

"Can you be there, too?"

After a hesitation, he said, "Me?"

"Well, yes. You are involved in your father's business, aren't you?"

286

"Sure, but . . ."

"Good. I'll be there around eight."

"What is this all about?"

"Eight o'clock, then, Perry."

I went to the safe in my office and took out my Smith and Wesson .38. I loaded it, dropped it into my jacket pocket, and walked out of my office. Zerk looked up.

"Where you going with that gun?" he said.

"It shows, huh?"

He shook his head back and forth, grinning. "You're going to get yourself into trouble, you know that?"

I shrugged. "I'm bringing the gun so I won't."

"So where are you going?"

"I'm going to pay a call on Ollie Weston."

"The stamp, eh?"

"Yes."

"You got it figured out?"

"I think so," I said. "I'll know more when I get back."

"And you're bringing a gun with you."

I nodded, a little sheepishly.

"Want to talk about it?"

"Not yet," I said. "Tell you what. Suppose I meet you later on? Maybe have a dish of shells at Marie's, couple bottles of Chianti. Say around ten?"

"Why don't I go with you?"

"No," I said. "That wouldn't work. I'll meet you at Marie's."

Chapter 16

The floodlights which hung in the eaves of the Weston mansion bathed the circular drive-around in warm, orange light and cast eerie shadows across the sweep of lawn. I drove through the front gate, which had been left open for me, parked my BMW directly in front of the entry, climbed the half-dozen wide steps to the big porch, and rang the bell.

I waited several moments before Perry opened the door. "Come on in," he said, stepping aside for me.

I brushed past him. "Where's Edwin?"

"Gave him the night off. He left right after dinner." Perry grinned. "Edwin has a lady friend, you know."

"Good for him."

"We're in the sitting room," said Perry, leading the way. Ollie was seated in his wheelchair at a big table near the window. To his right stood the wall-sized bookcase behind which lay his secret air-locked vault. From hidden speakers came a Sibelius symphony. Ollie had a shotgun opened on his lap. He was rubbing the metal parts of the gun with a rag. I recognized the pleasant odor of Hoppe's gun oil.

"Brady, my friend," he said when he saw me. "Long time. Here," he commanded, thrusting the gun at me. "Heft this."

I took the shotgun from him and lifted the stock gently to the barrels, snapping it shut. I admired the engraving along the side. The gold and ivory inlay depicted a setter on point. I raised it to my shoulder and swung it across the row of books. I dropped it, then lifted it to my shoulder again.

"A Parker," said Ollie. "Finest grade. Twenty-gauge. I've shot hundreds of quail with that gun. Thousands. In my better days. I had a plantation in Georgia, you know. Two thousand acres. Just for quail shooting."

"Get you a drink?" said Perry.

"No, thanks," I said.

"Dad?"

"No." Ollie rolled himself away from the table and swiveled his wheelchair around to face me. I broke open the shotgun and laid it on the table, then sat in a dark leather armchair. Perry perched on the arm of the chair beside mine. "So," said Ollie. "What brings you out? Not looking for a game of chess, are you?"

290

"No, Ollie. I want to update you on the Dutch Blue Error."

Ollie tossed his head. "Ah, well. It's gone, I know. No matter. Like I told you, it's no good to anybody unless they sell it to me anyway." He peered at me. "You haven't found it, have you?"

I ignored the question. "I have a story for you," I said. "Interested?"

Ollie shrugged his heavy shoulders. "You came all the way out here to tell me a story, I suppose I ought to listen."

"It concerns a man named Guillaume Lundi. Ring a bell?"

Ollie glanced at Perry, then jerked his shoulders again. "Go on," he said.

"Mr. Lundi served as a purchasing agent at an auction in Paris in April of 1967. He bought a valuable postage stamp. Then he flew to San Juan with the stamp, evidently to deliver it to his client. Guillaume Lundi was found in the hotel swimming pool with a broken neck. Suicide. They said he jumped from the balcony above the pool."

"I don't get it," said Perry.

"Your father does," I said to him. "On the ninth floor of the hotel, the room directly above the pool was registered to an American guest. A certain Mr. Grayson. Mr. Grayson was seen in the company of Mr. Lundi that evening." I turned to Ollie. "The Puerto Rican police were not very diligent. The hotel people wanted it handled quietly. By the time the body was found, Mr. Grayson had checked out. But Lundi didn't commit suicide, did he, Ollie?"

Ollie smiled at me. "Good for you, my boy." He chuckled. "You know, I didn't retain you to dredge up unfortunate incidents from my past. You are too damn persistent." He nodded. "Yes. That was I. Do you intend to reopen that case, Brady, like a dutiful officer of the court?"

"I don't understand," I said, "why you had to kill Guillaume Lundi."

Ollie shook his head. "I explained all that to you. The mystery of the stamp had to be nurtured. At all costs. That's all. Mr. Lundi prevented that." He raised his hands and let them fall, dismissing Guillaume Lundi. "You'll have a hell of a time making a case on that, you know."

Perry was staring at his father. "You killed a man?"

Ollie nodded. "It was quite necessary. Regrettable, but necessary. I lost my legs not long after that, you know. I've often wondered if that was some sort of divine retribution." He turned to me. "Why are you doing this, Brady? Why are you telling me this now?"

"It's part of the picture," I replied. "Let me continue. Mr. Schwartz, from whom you bought the stamp in Paris, made a point of finding out who Lundi delivered it to. It was no problem to figure out that Mr. Grayson was, in fact, Oliver Hazard Perry Weston. I have talked to Schwartz. At length."

"Ah," sighed Ollie softly. "That's how Sullivan – Shaughnessey, I believe his real name was – found out about me."

"Right. Schwartz sold him that information."

"Well," Ollie smiled, "I do hope you're not accusing me of murdering Shaughnessey. Or poor Albert. I've been parked right here." He thumped his dead legs with his fists.

"Yes. I know. But Perry has legs."

Ollie's head jerked around to stare at his son. "Him?"

"Don't listen to him," said Perry.

"You can correct me on the details, Perry, but this is how I figure you did it. You knew when I'd be going to the museum to get the stamp authenticated. You made a point of being there. Parked inconspicuously outside. You saw me and Zerk arrive, greet Albert. A few minutes later you saw us meet another man. Shaughnessey. Who you knew as

Sullivan, and who, you knew, owned the stamp. You saw us all go into the building together. You waited. When we came out, you followed Shaughnessey home. A couple nights later you went back there. You rang his bell. You told him who you were, that you were coming on behalf of your father about the stamp. That made sense. He let you in. How'm I doing so far?"

"Go on," said Perry.

"Okay. You told him you were prepared to purchase the stamp. Maybe you even brought money with you to show him. Now, Shaughnessey was a very cautious man. He must have thought it odd, this change of procedure. But your finding his house and going to him would've made him uneasy enough to be willing to consummate the deal, get it over with and get the Dutch Blue Error off his hands. So he fetched the stamp, you gave him the money, and he poured you each a drink to seal the bargain. The first blow probably killed him. But you couldn't take the chance. So you hit him two more times. You took the money back, took the stamp, and ransacked the place to make it appear to have been a burglary gone bad. You figured since no one knew he was the one who had the stamp, no one would link his murder to it. Or to you. You even broke the window at the back door. A nice, professional touch. The police believed it, and if Zerk hadn't happened to see Shaughnessey's picture in the paper, no one would ever have been any the wiser. You could have presented your father with the stamp later, having saved him a quarter of a million dollars. Or," I added, glancing at Ollie, "you could have waited until Ollie died. Then you would have had it all to yourself. Your own secret."

Ollie raised his eyebrows at his son. "You?"

Perry had been glaring at me throughout my recitation. Then his expression shifted. I saw a smile play on his lips. "Yes, me. I *was* going to give it to you. I got it for you."

"I'll be damned," muttered Ollie.

"You killed a man for a stamp," said Perry. "So did I."

"But that wasn't the end of it," I said. "Because you got a phone call from Albert Dopplinger. He wanted to speak to your father, but that was when Ollie was laid up, so he talked to you. And what he told you was upsetting. So you had to kill him, too."

"You killed Albert?"

"He's right. I had to."

"Yes," I said. "You had that one all planned. Albert played right into it. You agreed to meet him at his laboratory, where
295

he was going to show you the proof of what he told you. It was all in his notebook. You brought a gun with you. You chloroformed him, took his notebook, and shot him. Just about then you heard me at the door. You turned off the lights and hid. You saw me come in, you saw Schwartz come in behind me and use your chloroform on me, and then you saw Zerk come in and take me away. Then you slipped away, clean as a flute."

Ollie was shaking his head slowly back and forth. "Is that the way it was?"

"I didn't see Brady come in. I had left by then."

Ollie waved his hand. "Details. So you have the stamp."

"Yes."

"Well, Jesus, boy, go get it."

Perry nodded and left the room. Ollie looked at me. "Imagine that. I didn't think the boy had it in him."

"He's a murderer, Ollie. Are you proud of him?"

Ollie smiled. "He *did* something, didn't he?"

"Yes. He did something. That's true."

"So what's next, then?"

"Oh, come off it, Ollie. You know what's next."

I was standing in front of Ollie's

wheelchair. My back was to the doorway. I saw Ollie's eyes shift to look over my shoulder. I started to turn around. Too late, I felt Perry's hand on my jacket pocket and a sharp pain at the base of my spine.

"You didn't think I'd just walk out of here with you, did you?" said Perry, lifting my Smith and Wesson from my pocket. I turned. Perry had stepped back. My gun dangled carelessly from his left hand. The muzzle of the little hand-gun he held in his right was a black eye staring at me.

"Cut it out, Perry. You've performed your heroics. It's all over now. Why don't you just give me that?" I held out my hand. Perry smiled. The gun remained steady in his hand.

"Just sit down, there, in that chair. I can kill you, too."

I sat. "You don't think I'd come here like this without telling anyone, do you?" I said. "The police know all about this. They know I'm here."

He shook his head. "Somehow I doubt that. They wouldn't have let you come alone. Anyway, it's not your style. And I don't seem to have too many choices." He spoke to Ollie.

"Here's your stamp." Without taking his eyes from my face, and without moving his gun from its aim at the bridge of my nose, he handed an envelope to Ollie.

Ollie took it eagerly, lifted the unsealed flap, and gingerly reached in with his thumb and forefinger. Then he held up a tiny scrap of paper to the light. He narrowed his eyes to study it. "The duplicate Blue Error," he whispered. "This is it." He looked at Perry. "You have exceeded my fondest expectations. We must celebrate. Brandy. Cigars."

Perry smiled. Still watching me, he moved to a sideboard and poured brandy into three snifters with one hand. With the other, he kept the gun pointing at me. He handed one glass to Ollie and one to me. Then he took a silver case, flipped up the cover, and held it to his father. Ollie reached in and removed a slender cigar.

Perry stood by his father's shoulders, the automatic wedged into one hand, his own snifter of brandy in the other. Ollie lifted his glass.

"Again, Brady, let us drink to the Dutch Blue Error."

I shrugged and sipped with the two Weston men.

Ollie placed his glass on the table beside him. He still held the stamp in one hand. He put the cigar into his mouth and reached for a big silver lighter.

"Now I own two Dutch Blue Errors," he said slowly, rolling the cigar in his mouth. He held up the stamp again and squinted at it. "There's an interesting thing about stamps," he continued. "If, let us say, a million stamps of a particular issue existed, and each stamp was worth a dime, and one man owned every one of them, each stamp would bring no more than a dime on the market. Now, supposing there were only one of those stamps. And supposing it was worth a million dollars. And supposing the man who owned it suddenly came into possession of a second stamp – its duplicate. What do you think would be the value of each of those two stamps?"

Ollie stared at me.

"You asking me?" I said.

"Yes. See what you've learned."

"Each of them would be worth at least half a million, I suppose. More, probably, if you were able to maintain the mystery about them."

Ollie shook his head sadly. "Ah, no. Unfortunately, it doesn't work that way." He glanced at Perry, then returned his attention to me. "You see, what happens is that the very existence of the duplicate destroys the value of the original. It's no longer unique. Where there's one duplicate, there may be more. Now. I'm very glad to have this duplicate. Not because I want to own it. But simply because I want to be certain that nobody else ever will."

Ollie paused, flicked his lighter, and fired up his cigar. He rotated it slowly over the flame, then blew a great cloud of fragrant blue smoke at the ceiling, still holding the flaming lighter. "There is now a way that I can secure the uniqueness of my own Dutch Blue Error," he said softly.

"Hey! What are you doing?" said Perry suddenly. Then he said, "Jesus Christ! Don't do that!"

It was too late. Ollie delicately held the little stamp over the lighter until it burst into a tiny orange flame. He dropped it into an ashtray on the table beside him. The flame died out in a moment, and the duplicate Blue Error was a tiny mound of black ash.

"Thanks, Perry," said Ollie, smiling around the cigar in his mouth. "It wasn't much, true, but you *did* contribute something useful for a change."

Perry's eyes narrowed. "You son of a bitch," he whispered. "Now you've spoiled it all."

The report of Perry's automatic was

startlingly loud for so tiny a weapon. I saw Ollie Weston's head jerk, then sag onto his chest. A narrow, shiny red streak trickled slowly down his leathery neck from the black hole beneath his ear.

I leaped up and went to Ollie. I knelt in front of him and looked up into his face. His eyes were staring into his lap. His lips were drawn back over his teeth, which still clenched the smoldering cigar. I reached for his wrist, felt for his pulse, and held my fingers on it. It beat slowly and faintly.

I looked up at Perry, who was staring expressionlessly at Ollie. "He's still alive," I said.

Perry seemed transfixed. The gun in his hand was pointed at me.

I tried to take the cigar from Ollie's mouth. It broke off in his teeth. Then I felt again for his pulse. It seemed fainter and more irregular.

"For Christ's sake, get on the phone. Call an ambulance or something," I shouted at Perry. He continued to stare at his father. The gun did not waver in his hand.

Ollie blinked and groaned weakly. He lifted his hand a couple of inches from his lap and turned it so that his palm faced up. His eyelids flickered. He looked at me. I detected the crinkle of a smile. He wanted to tell me something. I put my ear to his mouth.

"A thousand damn quail," he whispered.

I looked into his face. He widened his eyes as if he wanted to say more. Then his pupils rolled up into his head, and his hand fell back into his lap. From deep in his big chest came a gagging groan. His powerful head lolled on his chest. I clutched at his wrist. There was no pulse.

I sat back on my heels and looked up at Perry. "He's dead."

Perry's eyes narrowed at me. He seemed to shiver. He closed his eyes tightly for a moment, and when he opened them they were clear and glittering. He motioned to me with his gun.

"Get over there," he said, his voice low and steady.

"You just killed your father, Perry," I said to him, trying to keep my own voice calm. "Why don't you just give me the gun, now."

I held out my hand carefully toward him. He took a quick step backward. "Yes," he said, watching me. "I did. I killed the bastard. I always knew he was a cruel son of a bitch. But I never thought he was stupid."

"You found Albert's notebook, didn't you?"

"Yes." Perry laughed. "Isn't that ironic,

him burning *that* stamp? He wouldn't listen to me. Never would. He always had to be right, never could admit that he might be wrong and *I* could be right. Well, he did his last cruel, stupid thing, didn't he?"

"Come on, Perry. Give me that gun. It's all over now."

Perry's eyes darted wildly around the room, then settled on me. He blinked, as if he were seeing me for the first time. Then he smiled.

"No," he said. "It's not over. Move over there."

At that moment a chime sounded from the front of the house. Perry's head jerked around.

"Jesus," he muttered. "The doorbell. Who the hell can that be?"

"Ask not," I said. "It tolls for thee."

"Shut up."

"The Fuller Brush man, perchance. Avon calling."

Perry jabbed at me with the gun. "Come on. We're getting out of here." He gestured toward the back of the house.

"Don't you think you should see who's at the door?"

"Why should I?"

"I told you, the police know I'm here."

Perry frowned for a moment. Then he

303

nodded. "Yeah, okay. We'll take a look. Let's see who it is. If you try anything, I'll shoot him, whoever it is. Do you understand?"

I nodded.

"I mean it. I'll kill him. I've got nothing to lose. Just do what I say. Let's go."

Perry directed me out of the room, through the grand hallway, and out into the big slate-tiled foyer by the front door. He gestured for me to stand beside the doorway, out of sight from anybody standing outside the door, but only a few feet from where Perry stood to open it.

He pulled the door open with his left hand. He held his right hand, with the gun in it, behind his back. I saw him smile.

"Yes?"

"This *is* the Weston house?" The voice belonged to Zerk. I wondered where all the police were.

"Yes. What can I do for you?"

"I'm looking for my friend. Brady Coyne. He told me he'd be here tonight."

"And you just happened to be in the neighborhood."

"More or less."

I saw Perry smile. "Sure. He's here. Come on in."

He stood back and opened the door all the

way. Zerk walked in. "I'm sorry to bother you at this hour, but . . ."

He saw me standing there, grinning foolishly at him. Then he saw the gun in Perry's hand. "Ah, shit," he mumbled.

Perry closed the door and gestured at Zerk to stand beside me. He kept waving the gun back and forth from Zerk to me and back to Zerk.

"You should have called the police," I said. "You trying to be some kind of hero?"

Zerk rolled his eyes. *"Me?"*

"Okay, so we're both dumb. But you should have called Kirk."

Zerk turned down the corners of his mouth. "Not likely."

"You guys shut up," said Perry. "Listen. We're going to leave here now. One of you tries something, the other one gets it. I mean it. Tell him, Brady."

"He means it."

"I've killed three people already."

"He's killed three people already," I said. "Including his old man."

Zerk turned to stare at me. I nodded.

"Christ!" he muttered.

"Put your hands on top of your heads and walk out that door," ordered Perry. "Go slow and stay close beside each other. Remember what I said."

"Just like the movies," I said.

"Japanese prisoners of war," added Zerk.

"I said, shut up," said Perry.

We moved out the door onto the big veranda. Zerk's little yellow Volkswagen was parked behind my white BMW in the circular drive. I looked for a police car. I listened for the thump of helicopters. There was nothing else out there. Just me and Zerk and a crazy man with a gun pointed at our backs.

I felt the muzzle of the gun poke my kidneys. "Okay," said Perry. "You get in and drive the white car. Remember, your friend is here with me. Just open the door slowly and slide in. Leave the door open."

I did as I was told. I heard Perry instruct Zerk, "And you. You open the back door. Just open it and step aside." Zerk obeyed. "Okay. Now you get in the front seat. Easy. Just open the door and get in. Leave the door open."

Zerk slid in beside me.

At that instant I heard a familiar voice. "Hold it right there, Weston. Drop the gun."

I glanced around and saw Leo Kirk step out from the shadows near the veranda. He was crouched, his feet wide apart. The gun he clutched in his two hands was extended

306

straight in front of him. It was aimed at Perry.

The rest happened in an instantaneous flash. Two gunshots, sudden and ear-shattering. A moment's pause, then a third shot. And then a voice, small and wondering, a moan combined with a sigh. "Oh." And silence.

Leo Kirk moved forward, his weapon still gripped in both hands and pointed at Perry Weston's crumpled body. Zerk and I climbed out of the car and stood with Kirk, staring down at Perry. Kirk knelt, held a finger against Perry's throat, then looked up at me. He shook his head.

"He's dead."

I nodded.

The cop stood up, shrugged his shoulders, and walked into the house. His gun still dangled from his hand.

Zerk and I went and sat on the front steps. "You *did* call the cops," I said.

"Yeah. I don't have to like them to know when discretion, as they say, is the better part of valor. Kirk's parked out in the street. We decided if you were in trouble, we'd have a better chance of helping you out if the cops didn't start pounding on the door."

"Good thinking."

"That was Kirk's idea."

307

"You took quite a risk."

He shrugged. "It's what I seem to be doing these days. It worked."

I stared out at Perry Weston's body. "In a way, it worked."

A few minutes later Kirk came back from inside the house and sat heavily beside us. "There's another body in there," he said.

"I know," I said. "Perry did that."

"I called an ambulance and all the rest. They're on their way. We've got to wait. So why don't you tell me what happened?"

So I told him.

When I finished my recitation, Kirk stared at me. "The Lone Ranger rides again, eh?"

I glanced at Zerk. "I left my faithful Indian companion home."

"Ha, ha," said Zerk sarcastically. "Another ethnic slur."

"Why the hell didn't you call me?" said Kirk.

"It was all supposition," I said. "Just a story I put together in my head. I would've looked like an ass if I'd been wrong."

"You didn't look so smart when we got here," said Zerk mildly.

"Besides," I continued, ignoring him, "I didn't figure there was enough for you to get a warrant, so what could you do?"

"That's for us to decide," said Kirk.

"I *am* an attorney, you know." It sounded more defensive than I'd intended. "In my judgment..."

"Okay, okay. So you're an attorney. What I still don't understand is why Perry shot the old man."

"Several reasons. First, Ollie never respected Perry, never gave him encouragement, never acknowledged that Perry was a man. Treated him like a boy. Made it clear he didn't trust him. I don't imagine there was much love there. Ollie was not a demonstrative man in that respect. And remember – Ollie brought up Perry himself. With the help from butlers and nannies and so forth. Perry's mother swallowed a bottle of pills when he was a baby. So you can figure it out."

"Yeah, yeah. All that Oedipal stuff. Still..."

"Okay, the stamp. Perry finally had proved himself, he figured. Just like his daddy. He went out and killed a couple of people, stole the stamp, and would once and for all show his pop he was a real man, deserving full respect. He made the grand presentation, and Ollie spat in his face by burning it."

"I still don't get it," said Kirk. "He burned the duplicate. But he still had the original stamp. Seems to me Perry had done a good thing, and both he and Ollie knew it, and Perry should have understood that burning the stamp made sense."

I shook my head. "There's the irony. The stamp Ollie burned was the original Dutch Blue Error. The *only* Dutch Blue Error. Not a duplicate. There was no duplicate Blue Error. Ollie's stamp, the one he owned all those years, was a fake. Shaughnessey's stamp was the only real one. So Ollie burned the real stamp and kept the fake. Perry knew that. Ollie didn't."

"But Albert said . . ." began Zerk.

"Albert knew," I answered. "When we took the stamps to him, he saw immediately that the stamp Ollie had always owned was a fake, and the one Shaughnessey brought was the genuine article. Naturally, Albert wasn't going to let Shaughnessey know that. He was loyal to Ollie, and he knew that it would change everything. So he waited, and then called Ollie to tell him. Except Perry answered the phone. So Albert told Perry. He didn't realize, of course, that Perry had already killed Shaughnessey for the stamp, or that, in Perry's warped little brain, all secrets had to be protected – at any price. Perry agreed to meet Albert – to see the evidence. Then he killed Albert. To maintain

310

the secret of the stamp. And he took Albert's notebook, which contained the evidence. And when he handed the stamp to Ollie this evening, he was about to make the grand announcement that he, Perry, had done what Ollie himself hadn't been able to do – get the real Dutch Blue Error. But Ollie deprived him of that great satisfaction."

"He burned the stamp."

"Yes," I said. "And that's when Perry broke. All that was left was all the pent-up frustration and rage. A whole lifetime of it."

"So he shot him."

"Yes."

"And all those years Ollie's stamp was a fake," mused Zerk. "How could that be?"

"Schwartz did it. He owned the original and offered it for sale to Ollie back in sixty-seven. So far, so good. But then he got greedy. He had a fake made – a good fake, of course, using one of the original orange stamps and carefully altering the color to make it blue. Same old paper, and so forth. Same old stamp, actually, except for the color. It'd take an expert like Albert to detect it, and even then it'd be hard to do without the genuine Blue Error to compare it with. So Schwartz felt pretty safe. He kept the original stamp and sold Ollie the fake. To make it work, he gave Ollie the papers of authentication for the real stamp. And last winter, nearly twenty years later, he had the chance to sell the genuine stamp to Shaughnessey, who traveled in the same circles as Schwartz, and who was not beneath cutting a few ethical corners to turn over a buck. Schwartz didn't tell Shaughnessey what a bargain he was getting. He didn't need to. He gave Shaughnessey a good price on the stamp plus Ollie's name, and sat back to let the chips fall wherever."

"I'll be damned," breathed Kirk.

"So when I heard all that from Schwartz, all I had to do was to try to figure out who could've learned it. I eliminated everyone but Perry. But it was still a guess. I came here hoping I could smoke him out."

"Which you did. Damn near got yourself smoked, too," said Zerk.

"Both of us," I said.

Sirens sounded in the distance, and a minute later several official vehicles skidded into the driveway, their red and blue lights flashing eerily. Kirk stood up and went to talk with the men who piled out of the cars. Some moved into the house. Others gathered around Perry's body. Zerk and I remained seated on the steps, ignored by the others. I lit a Winston and leaned back to watch.

After a while Kirk wandered over and

stood in front of us. "You guys can go, if you want. I'll be in touch with you, Brady. Lots of questions, but they can wait."

Zerk and I stood up. I held out my hand to Kirk. "Thanks," I said.

"That was my first," he said, his eyes searching mine. "The first man I ever killed."

"You had to, man," said Zerk. "No choice."

"Yeah. You're right. I had no choice. Still..."

I squeezed Kirk's hand. He nodded to me, then turned and walked up the steps into the house. Zerk and I climbed into our cars and drove home.

EPILOGUE

I had my chair swiveled around so that I could look out my office window at the gray November cityscape. The fountains of the Copley Square Plaza had been turned off for the winter, and the planes and angles of the concrete mall looked cold and bleak. Old Trinity Church, that ancient and elegant pile of rock, faced across to the Library. Old South Church watched from across the way. To my right, just beyond my vision, loomed the Hancock Tower, and off to my left rose The Pru, all fifty-two stories of it. Everything was painted in gloomy shades of battleship gray.

I was pondering the relative merits of lunch at Jake Wirth's with Charlie McDevitt versus a lengthy and leisurely afternoon with Douglas Segrue amid the old leather and mahogany paneling of the Algonquin Club.

Segrue had business for me. Something about some property near the University of Massachusetts campus in Amherst that he wanted to buy and convert into condominiums. The Algonquin Club would serve lobster bisque and Oysters Rockefeller and dust-dry martinis. Doug would pay. We might even be lured into a penny-a-point bridge game.

Charlie had a joke for me. The one about the guy with a trained alligator. Charlie chuckled over the phone at the thought of the punch line. I hadn't heard it. It would cost me the price of his platter of German potato salad and a couple of steins of dark beer to hear it.

It was a tough choice. But, hell, we lawyers are paid to make the tough choices.

There was a light rap on the door.

"Come on in, Zerk," I said.

I heard the door open and close. I didn't turn around.

"Cold out there," he said.

"Winter's coming," I agreed.

"You busy?"

"I am deep in the throes of legal analysis. *Stare decisis, amicus curiae, writs of certiorari,* all that stuff."

Zerk cleared his throat. "Thought you'd like to know," he said. "I passed the bar."

I rotated around to face him, stood, and extended my hand to him. "Hey, now. That is good news. Congratulations."

We shared an old-fashioned handshake.

Zerk sat in the chair opposite my desk. "We've got to talk," he said.

"I was going to say the same thing."

"Now that I'm a full-fledged attorney . . ."

"Let me talk first," I said.

He raised his eyebrows and nodded.

"Julie's due back the first of the year, you know, and, well . . ."

"I know," he interrupted. "Don't make it tough on yourself. I know I've got to look for a job. It's okay. I didn't want to be a secretary all my life, anyway."

"What I wanted to say was this," I said. "I think I could use a partner around here. A junior partner. There's plenty of work – as much as I want to take on. No end to people's problems, you know. It'd be good to have someone to work with. And – hell, Zerk. You want to come work for me, or what?"

"I was wondering if you were going to ask," he said softly.

"Does that mean yes?"

"No. That means no, Brady. I'm sorry."

"Look. It doesn't have to be forever, you know. Just to get you on your feet, make some contacts, earn a couple bucks. I'm sincere about the offer."

"It's nice of you. I'm flattered. I know you'd rather work alone."

"Working with you would be better than working alone."

"It's not what I want."

"Oh."

"Nothing personal. But, hell, I don't trust myself. The money, the contracts, all the soft cases. I'm afraid I'd be seduced. I want to do something that's real, that makes a difference. Helping rich people stay rich – or get richer – that's not for me. That's not my idea of a career." He stared at me. "No offense intended."

I shrugged. "It's up to you. But you ought to think it over."

"I have," he said. "It was easy. I want to *do* something. I don't want just some law practice."

"Hell, Zerk. It's just a career. It's a job, that's all. Listen. My law practice isn't the most important thing in my life, you know."

His dark eyes stared sorrowfully at me. "What is, then?"

I laughed. "Having lunch with Charlie McDevitt. Drinking dark beer and finding out about the trained alligator. Right now, that's the most important thing in my life." I stood up and reached across my desk to clap his shoulder. "I wish you well. Perhaps we'll meet in court one day."

He nodded and grinned. "Perhaps we will. And I'll whip your tail."

"Whether you do or not, you'll know you've been in a tussle."

"Believe it," he said.

Talcum snow as fine as smoke swirled on the sidewalks and misted through the headlights of passing cars. Deborah clutched my bicep with both of her hands and with squinted eyes savored the season's first snowfall on her face. Tiny droplets, melting on contact with her cheeks and chin, made her face glow.

We descended the five steps to the entrance of Marie's. Inside, Deborah shook herself like a golden retriever that had fetched a stick from the water. We hung up our coats, then followed a lithe, blue-jeaned waitress to a table against the brick wall. A candle burned in its wine-bottle holder. Deborah grinned at me through the flame.

"So the weather gods have blessed us again with a little demonstration," she said.

"Or cursed us."

"It's not even Thanksgiving. Looks like a long winter."

The slim waitress produced a fat bottle of Mateus roŝe, which she placed in the middle of the table. "Compliments of Marie," she said. "Our specials tonight are tortellini –

which is pasta stuffed with white meats, prosciutto, mortadella, Parmesan cheese, and various herbs and spices, served with our Bolognese sauce." The girl grinned. "It's delicious. Also egg fettuccine with tomato and basil sauce. Equally great." The girl pointed at the blackboard on the wall. "Our regular things are up there. Would you like a minute to think about it?"

I raised my eyebrows to Deborah. She shook her head. "I won't be able to make up my mind any better in a minute. I'll try the first thing you said."

"The tortellini," said the girl.

"Yes."

"Then I'll have the fettuccine," I said. "And a salad for each of us. Just the lettuce with your house dressing."

She smiled and swiveled away.

I poured each of us a glass of wine. Deborah held hers to me. "To your health."

We clicked glasses and sipped.

Deborah peered into her wine glass. "You've been avoiding me."

"No. Not really."

She shrugged.

"We've talked on the phone. When I can get past Darlene, and your mechanical answering machine. I've been busy. Work piled up."

She nodded.

Our salads arrived. We ate them in silence. I refilled our wine glasses.

"I've been doing a lot of thinking," said Deborah, her eyes focused on the flame of the candle.

"Me too."

"About us."

I nodded.

"We – we never did get along that well, really, you know?"

I smiled and didn't answer. She toyed with her fork. When she looked up, her silver eyes were wide and serious.

"I learned a lot from you, you know. About myself, about marriage, and . . ." She stopped.

"And what?"

She sighed. "I've decided to go back to Philip."

"I see."

"Oh, it's a long story."

"You don't have to tell me."

She shrugged. "Yes. Well, anyway, we've got to give ourselves a chance, that's all. I don't want to – to make a mistake."

"The way I did."

"Yes."

"I'm happy for you, then," I said.

"Thank you."

"But I'm not happy for me."

"We wouldn't have worked out." She leaned forward. "You know that, don't you?"

"Yes, I know. That's not it."

"Brady, I'm sorry."

I smiled. I thought of the little speech I had prepared for the occasion. The age difference. The dissipation of my child-rearing energies. My slothful housekeeping habits. The enthusiasm with which I avoided chores like lawnmowing and driveway shoveling, and wallpaper hanging. The importance of my twice-weekly golf matches. The long weekends I spent on distant trout rivers. The arbitrary hours I spent in the office.

I'm fixed in my ways, Deborah, the speech read. No flexibility left. Anyway, there's this woman in my life. Known her for a long time. Was even married to her, once. The married part didn't work, never could, but...

I folded up my little speech and tucked it back into the hip pocket of my mind. Deborah was staring across the table at me, concern etched into two vertical lines between her eyes.

"Don't worry about me," I said. "I'll be okay."

The publishers hope that this book has given you enjoyable reading. Large Print Books are specially designed to be as easy to see and hold as possible. If you wish a complete list of our books, please ask at your local library or write directly to: John Curley & Associates, Inc. P.O. Box 37, South Yarmouth Massachusetts, 02664